Critical Acclaim for Brigid Brophy

'Brief, distinguished, strikingly original . . . because of its strangeness it places an admiring reviewer in a quandary. One wants to say enough about this fascinating book to arouse the curiosity of those readers to whom it will surely delight. But to say too much would be a pity, for it offers, among other pleasures, the very keen one of discovery . . . A brilliantly accomplished small book which widens out into large meanings'—*Herald Tribune*

'Writing with that kind of brilliance which makes the rest of the world seem to step back into shadow, Brigid Brophy makes her comedy out of the conflicting impulses in the outward urge in man and his ape ancestor'—*Alex Hamilton, Books and Bookmen*

'Elegant and pleasing in its dry wit'—*Times Literary Supplement*

'Brilliantly written'—*Daily Telegraph*

'A pointed and amusing satire'—*Time Magazine*

BRIGID BROPHY

was born in London in 1929, daughter of the novelist John Brophy. She was educated at St. Paul's Girls' School and St. Hugh's College, Oxford. In 1954 she married Michael Levey, who was the Director of the National Gallery from 1973 to 1986. He was knighted in 1981. They have a daughter and three grandchildren. In 1984 Brigid Brophy developed multiple sclerosis, a progressive and disabling neurological affliction.

Hackenfeller's Ape was published in 1953 and awarded the Cheltenham Festival Prize for a first novel in 1954. It was followed by *The King of a Rainy Country* (1956, also published by Virago), *Flesh* (1962), *The Finishing Touch* (1963), *The Snow Ball* (1964), *In Transit* (1969), *The Adventures of God in His Search for the Black Girl* (1973) and *Palace Without Chairs* (1978).

In addition to her series of brilliant fictions, Brigid Brophy has written plays and many non-fiction works, of which perhaps her most famous is *Mozart the Dramatist*. This first appeared in 1964, and a revised edition was issued in 1988 to wide acclaim. She was one of the founders of Writers Action Group, which successfully campaigned for the establishment in Britain of Public Lending Right for authors. She is a member of the Labour Party and of the National Secular Society. She has held office in the Writers' Guild of Great Britain, a non-party-political trade union affiliated to the T.U.C., of which she was appointed an Honorary Life Member in 1991, and in the British Copyright Council. She is a vice-president of the National Anti-Vivisection Society and is known for her abiding and impassioned championing of animal rights.

Awards also include the *London Magazine* prize for prose (1962) and the 1985 Tony Godwin award.

VIRAGO
MODERN
CLASSIC

NUMBER

370

Brigid Brophy

HACKENFELLER'S APE

Published by VIRAGO PRESS Limited 1991
20–23 Mandela Street, Camden Town, London NW1 0HQ

First published in Great Britain in 1953 by Hart Davis

*A CIP catalogue record for this book
is available from the British Library*

Printed in Great Britain by
Cox & Wyman Ltd. Reading, Berks

In April 1991 *Hackenfeller's Ape*, my first novel, proved to be prophetic. After I was sent down (expelled from Oxford University), I shared a flat in North London with a friend, from which we heard the lions roaring from London Zoo. That redoubled my hatred of zoos.

Brigid Brophy, 1991

All the characters in this novel are fictitious;
so is the species Hackenfeller's Ape,
but not the species Homo Sapiens

CONTENTS

I PREDICAMENT OF AN APE

Sunday

RADIANT and full-leafed, the Park was alive with the murmuring vibration of the species which made it its preserve. The creatures, putting off timidity at the same time as winter drabness, abounded now with no ascertainable purpose except to sun themselves. Their seasonal brilliance — scarlet, sky-blue, yellow — interspersed the deep, high-summer greenness of the foliage. The ground, too hard to receive their spoors, shook beneath games that revealed a high degree of social organisation. Elsewhere the grass lay folded back, shewing where solitaries of the race had eased themselves into forms. On the gravel paths, scuffles and hoots gave evidence of courting rites; and in every part the characteristic calls of the kind lay clear and pleasant upon the vivid air.

In the central meadow they were playing cricket. Westward, the shouts and splashes of the boating lake lingered, like gentle explosions, above the expanse of shallow water. North-west, the canal stood black and transparent like indian ink, between banks mottled by sun. Once or twice a day a boat slowly passed, silencing the fish in their continual scratching of the surface, and propelling towards the sides tangible hanks of water, curled into wreaths, braids and pigtails. North of the Park, a tarmac road had been laid over the landscape. At all times it was arid; this weather made it torrid. A row of cars was already here, standing outside a wire-bound entrance which led to the only section of the Park that could not be enjoyed free. The bodywork of the cars was scorching. Their windscreens threw off, at a squinting angle, dazzling blots of light. Some belonged to people privileged to go in when the general public was excluded and who were at this moment inside. Others belonged to members of the public who, misinformed, had come too early; who had been refused at the turnstiles; who now had to fill in time and eat their parcelled luncheons elsewhere. The children were the most resentful of the contretemps, sulky because their parents had proved not to be omnipotent. They resisted as they were pulled away: to gain time, they gazed upward as they went, pretending they could not walk straight, staring at an aeroplane that was doubling to and fro in the sky.

These were the young of a species which had laid out the Park with an ingenuity that outstripped the beaver's; which, already the most dextrous of the land animals, had acquired greater endurance under the sea than the whale and in the air had a lower casualty rate for its journeys than migrating birds. This was, moreover, the only species which imprisoned other species not for any motive of economic parasitism but for the dispassionate parasitism of indulging its curiosity.

That curiosity, however, was not to be indulged on Sunday before half-past two. The adults pulled the children on, past street vendors of orangeade and sticky bags of plums, who were already waiting for the crowds to arrive in earnest. Two or three old men, hoping to capitalise the guilt the adults must feel in denying the children, dangled dirty woollen caricatures of dogs and lambs on the end of a string, or thrust upon the mothers toy windmills with violently-coloured plastic sails, which there was no wind to turn.

It was a hot, flawless Sunday early in September.

Within the enclosure, Professor Clement Darrelhyde sat on an iron bench, quietly singing the Countess's cavatina from the second act of *Figaro's Marriage*.

> *"Porgi, amor, qualche ristoro*
> *Al mio duolo, a' miei sospir!*
> *O mi rendi il mio tesoro*
> *O mi lascia almen morir!"*

A soprano aria: so he sang falsetto. His voice was true but spindly, rather like a harpsichord; which made it almost exactly in period.

> *"Grant, O Love, some recompense*
> *To my sorrow, to my sighs!"*

He sang to the accompaniment of an aeroplane's noise, miles above, and for a moment he craned up to watch the vapour trail deposited on the sky. Perfect cricketing weather, perfect boating weather, this was also perfect flying weather. The Professor admired aeronautics, with its vapour trails and parachutes, and its discovery of cloudscape seen from above; the only achievement of his own century which he would compare with Mozart's music.

He brought his nose down and flattened out, resuming the vigil he kept over the opposite side of the path. There were few passers-by to cut off his vision, and none of them noticed him or the womanish noise he was uttering. They came bounding along, absorbed in their own energies and sense of privilege. They scrutinised the outlandish scene at large, anxious to

13

miss none of its wonders, questing for creatures more melodramatic than the Professor.

He was here on business — observation. What he had come to observe, however, and had fully expected to observe every day for three weeks, was not happening. Meanwhile, he sang.

He enjoyed the sunshine on his face and the patterns of the hot white dust at his feet.

"Al mio du-o-lo, a' miei sos-pir!"

The persistence of the aeroplane's noise, however, reminded him of an uneasiness in himself. Uneasiness seemed to be the background of all ruminations belonging to the twentieth century, just as all its landscapes were presided over, somewhere in the distance, by an aeroplane. The beauty of the flying machine was neutral. Carrying bombs or peace it left the choice, almost belligerently, to Man.

> *"Either restore to me my treasure*
> *Or let me at least die."*

Beneath all the blooming and splendid scents of this most assured time of year, there was another which reached the Professor: an odour shabby, seedy, somehow disgraceful: the smell of the caged animals.

Something moved on the far side of the path. The Professor sprang up, and approached the cage.

A false alarm. The male monkey, with that disregard of his own dignity which, rather than his physical appearance, marked him as non-human, had stood up to scratch his buttocks and then once more squatted down on them. Nothing else had changed. The two animals were still at opposite sides of their small cage, still unmoving, presenting to one another a disgruntled three-quarters profile.

In irritation, the Professor tapped the metal label fixed on the bars.

HACKENFELLER'S APE

Anthropopithecus Hirsutus Africanus

♂ ♀

Percy and *Edwina*

Hackenfeller had been (the Professor half knew, half assumed) a sober Dutchman who, exploring into Central Africa some time during the nineteenth century, had come upon a species not previously recorded. It was the same size as the gorilla, but in appearance and character nearer the chimpanzee. In captivity it moved on all fours; but in the jungle, as Hackenfeller had noted, it ran erect with its hands holding on to branches overhead. Children sometimes used a similar method when they learned to walk, but in the adult man it was forgotten until he had to relearn it in crowded buses and trains.

In Central Africa Hackenfeller's Ape was not rare, and not difficult to take alive. Almost any pretty and succulent fruit would lure it into a trap. In Europe it thrived but seldom mated. Any collector who wanted a pair of the apes had to incur the expense of sending for them south of the Equator. Accordingly there was only one cage here labelled "Hackenfeller's Ape": and this label, with a few like it in other zoos, was perhaps the

15

Dutchman's only memorial on the face of the earth — unless in some jungle clearing the largest of a few decaying huts still bore, scarcely legible, whatever the Dutch was for "Hackenfeller's Mission" or "Hackenfeller's Medical Institute".

After Hackenfeller had come London zoologists of the Professor's own kind. Working on specimens alive and dead, they had established that the eyesight of Hackenfeller's Ape, and the composition, temperature and pressure of its blood, came closer to the human model than those of any other animal. They had allotted to the species its place in the Evolutionary progress, and had devised its Latin name. One of them had inadvertently graced it with the proudest of old Roman titles: and knocking on the metal plate, gazing into the concrete cage, flooded yellow by the sun, the Professor felt a plumed and helmeted shadow fall across his mind at the memory of Scipio Africanus.

Ducking under the barrier which stood a foot or so from the cage, he approached so near that nothing but bars divided him from the animals. There they sat, ♂ and ♀, forced by their confinement into a resentful communion. If the Chimpanzees' Tea Party, which sometimes took place on a nearby lawn, was a rollicking caricature of human social life, here was a satire on human marriage. Separated by the yard or two that was the extent of their cage, not looking at one another, tensed, and huffy, Percy and Edwina might have been sitting at a breakfast table.

Perhaps apprehension of something like this had prevented the Professor himself from marrying: though he had never been assured that the woman existed who would have taken him.

"Porgi, Amor . . ."

16

he sang sadly, and was transported into another era, another sex.

He became the middle-aged Countess, tragically and with dignity calling on Love to restore her treasure — the affections of her Count. His voice did duty for a full, womanly voice: his scraggy body stepped into the body of a mature soprano — a body so magnificently weighted down that all its actions must be performed slowly, graciously and with stately mien. Was not this stagecraft? Turning the cumbrousness of ripe sopranos to dramatic advantage, Mozart had made his Countess tragic in the very fact that her waist was thickening while her hands remained tiny and manicured, and in the very fact that she could not compete, for the Count, with her own serving maid. Out of the strutting gait of fat-bellied bassi Mozart had created Figaro: conceited, pragmatic, a man with an air to him. To accompany the strut he had written the martial bars that rounded off *Non Più Andrai*: and when, the Professor wondered, in all human existence had the curtain of a first act come down on such ringing exhilaration as *Non Più Andrai* and the curtain of a second act risen on such tenderness as *Porgi Amor?*

Irritated again, he tapped the label again, this time using Figaro's own rhythm. For the world did not do Mozart justice. Day by day people saw his charm, and missed his depth, his grandeur, his religion. They belittled him as a light composer, and praised such shallow things as——

"Rossini!" the Professor cried aloud, in contemptuous comparison.

The male monkey turned his face upward, sympathising with the Professor's indignation, although he did not understand its cause. Indeed, he was half worried lest he himself had offended. The female monkey only stared at the Professor. If he felt indig-

17

nation, she was pleased. If it could have entered her mind that she had caused it, she would be more pleased still.

"Not you," the Professor said aloud to Percy, "but Rossini."

The animal was almost reassured. He no longer looked direct at the Professor. But there was something imploring still in his attitude, just as there had been something pathetic in his prompt adoption of Rossini's guilt to himself. He seemed to demand from the Professor some intellectual illumination. He sought enlightenment of his torment in prison.

The Professor had for a long time hedged, declining to admit there was torment, refusing to stand in the receiving position of this enquiring relationship, disinvolving himself from the monkeys' affairs.

At the time when he began his regular visits, he would have found it hard to distinguish Percy and Edwina from any other pair of Hackenfeller's Apes. He was superficially amused to watch them chase one another from the outdoor half of their cage to the indoor part, tucked away at the back and out of sight, and then from the indoor part out again. They used the full extent of the cage as a cubic area: their chases went also up and down, and up and down diagonally. Sometimes they shewed boredom, the consequence of play, and would fret for a moment; then one of them would invent a new game with the rubber tyre that was suspended from their ceiling.

The professional part of his mind observed that the animals were in good condition: not over-verminous; skin and eyes healthy in appearance. Evidently their diet and the space allotted to them were adequate.

In the second week of his vigil their activities had begun to slow down. He found them approaching one another about some matter more important than the rubber tyre. They held conferences, and jabbered in each other's ears. All that was puppyish in them was ousted by a tension, a single-minded concentration, which could overtake only mature bodies.

There was no record that any white man had witnessed the mating of Hackenfeller's Ape. There was, however, a native tradition on the subject. Conscientiously, Hackenfeller had taken notes about something he could never see himself, since he never travelled in the jungle without an entourage. The Negroes who claimed to have seen it had all been alone, and had had the patience not to frighten the animals.

Hackenfeller's notes had been translated into German. From German they had been translated, after fifty years' delay, into English: and it was in this translation that the Professor had read the account, which might or might not be trustworthy, of a ceremonial so poetic, so apparently conscious that, if it were true, it must mark a stage between the highest beast and Man.

Late August and September were known to be the season. The Professor began watching. He could safely ignore those times when the zoo was full. He came only for an hour or two after opening time on weekdays and all morning on Sundays. He was not worried what might happen at night. The monkeys, unlike Man, had not banished this act to the dark.

When he observed the mating fervour seize the apes, he came as near as his temperament allowed to ambition, though scarcely to personal ambition. He could not expect even such a memorial as Hackenfeller's. The utmost would be a footnote in every future monograph on the species. What he hoped was to replace the confused, anonymous, undated tradition, which had been preserved among untrained minds, by a couple of sentences, packed and precisely descriptive.

However, the negotiations between Edwina and Percy were unfruitful, and the two had settled implacably into their opposite corners. From the first it was plain that the female was willing. The scruple, the inhibition of will, whatever it was, lay in the male. The Professor had felt impatient. The animal was healthy enough: why didn't it do what it was in its nature to do and at the same time benefit science? The female would whimper in her corner, and in the early days the Professor's sympathy was for her. Sometimes she sallied out and grasped Percy round the waist. He with impatience, often with disgust, would push her away. She would retire, wounded in her pride; but her desire for him and, ultimately, her hope, remained obstinate and unextinguished. She would fix her eyes on him, and concentrate.

Nonetheless, Percy's rebuttal was more than an animal gesture. He disengaged himself with something the Professor could only call gentleness. He seemed to be perplexed by his own action, and imposed on his muscles a control and subtlety hardly proper to his kind. His own puzzling need to be fastidious appeared to distress him as much as Edwina's importunity. After their entanglements he would turn his melancholy face towards her and seem to be breaking his heart.

The more he frustrated Edwina, the more Percy suffered for his muteness. In desperation he would come to the front of the cage and stare out. In the worst moments, he clambered a little way up the bars, and clung there bitterly.

It was then that the Professor entered a relationship with the monkeys. At first he simply crooned to Percy, because the sound soothed the pain — usually something from *Figaro's Marriage*. Then he had begun to talk. Incapable of baby-language, he offered precise, intellectual statements of consolation.

The scruple had come first: the Professor was sure he was not the cause of Percy's inhibition. But once he had felt it, Percy sought enlightenment. Why should he refrain from what he so evidently desired? (After Edwina had touched him, the Professor had seen, he quivered.) It was to the Professor that he addressed his appeal.

He learned first to be familiar, and to shew that he was familiar, with many of Mozart's airs. Then he learned to connect indignation with the name Rossini. For Rossini, as the Professor explained to him, had been born in the year after Mozart's death, and had dared to take the Almaviva household, known and dear to the Professor in its very gilt mirrors, powder closets and painted screens, and purport to shew its early history — the wooing, in their youth, of the Count and Countess. As if that was not included, a retrospective microcosm, in the Countess's three falling syllables: te-so-ro! He had called Mozart's Countess (the Contessa, the Gräfin — the Professor loved her in all possible tongues) by her Christian name: and had made her into a pert chit. The Count he had turned into a sweet, pie-faced, insipid hero, and had forced up his voice into a high, romantic tenor. Mozart's Count, on the other hand, even as he pursued his wife's maid, remained a Man. As for the maid——

"You need not think," the Professor had said into the cage, "that Susanna is a hussy. It is Mozart's triumph not to have made her a hussy."

Not one word did the monkey understand. Something perhaps reached him, hazily, of these ideals that occupied the Professor's thoughts, the ideals of a proper Man and a proper Woman. He groped after their meaning. How did they differ from a male monkey and a female monkey? How were they related to his own refusal to do what Edwina desired?

21

What the animal loved was not only the import of the words but the gift of words for its own sake. Finding himself insufficient to Edwina's occasions, he felt guilt: and he received an inkling that fluency in words might have at once explained and expiated his guilt. But, being dumb, he could only gaze at her with apology, until she was sufficiently encouraged to approach him again. Expecting a repulse, she came clumsily. She made herself repulsive; and Percy again repulsed her.

It was an indisputable scientific fact that Percy would never be able to speak. Yet it seemed no less indisputable, and no less to be established by science, that had he been able to live five hundred years he would have learnt. Here was an animal discontent with his monkeydom, already exercising the first characteristic of Man, which Man had never satisfactorily explained, self-restraint. Love in Edwina was thwarted from without, and it made her blunt. It sharpened Percy and pressed his energies to higher and higher things, because the discipline was self-chosen. The Professor discoursed to him on the struggles and failures, the aeons of Miocene and Pleistocene time, which had been necessary to bring him to this point, where not only his eyesight but his mental vision flickered on the verge of being human.

Percy was mal-adapted to being an ape; yet here, as at every stage of Evolution, the puzzle posed itself: why, among many mal-adapted creatures, most went under while a few went up.

Percy, bounded by his cage, had not seen and could not imagine the other species displayed in the Zoo. He could not recognise in them the footprints of his own ancestry. Time past meant nothing to him, least of all time recorded in compressed millennia, in fossils and rocks. Nevertheless, he came to know the word "Evolution" from its recurrence in the Professor's musings. From it he gained some notion of an indescribable effort through time, and the notion of his own obligation to press himself, with similar effort, beyond the limits of his nature and experience. He did not know what the Professor was urging him to reach; but he had some feeling that his reward would be to share with the Professor that kingdom outside the cage, which he only mistily saw, but where, it appeared to him, the Professor moved free and fluent.

"Courage," the Professor said. "Courage, my friend."

Percy frowned. His whole body became rigid with trying. Quite without literacy, he had no conception where one word ended and the next began, but by perseverance, worrying the syllables to make them yield up their virtue, he could distinguish "Evolution". "Mozart" and — most recently — "friend".

Seeing him intent, silent, flexed, Edwina let out a half second's chatter. Percy started. The vision on the tip of his mind was jerked back. It was now in limbo, whence he might or might not recall it next time the Professor chanced to speak the words.

On that chance Percy was dependent. He leaned on the Professor's intellect. Another man might have taught him jazz tunes and the names of the planets. Because the Professor's mind ranged in time rather than space, Percy's mind groped through time after him. Unable to reproduce the sounds, he could not even initiate the ideas. He had to wait till the Professor suggested them.

His chance lost, Percy turned on Edwina his most pitiable countenance.

Hoping to comfort him, the Professor drew an apple out of his pocket. At once there was less bulk to his figure. The thin, stained tweed suit he was unseasonably wearing fell into creases, and more nearly revealed how little flesh there was on his flanks.

He dusted off some tobacco and passed the apple through the bars. However, Percy was too agonised: he stared at the apple as if it was offensive.

The Professor persisted, moving the apple an inch closer.

Percy shifted his head, insulted. The Professor withdrew his arm. Percy moved towards him again, either to shew he felt no ill will, or else because he had forgotten the whole incident already.

Moving down the path, the Professor gave the apple to Edwina, and made contact with her hand — horny black at the palm, flushing deep rose at the tips — as she greedily took it.

She bit into the apple, and moved back a pace or two, seeking refuge in the depth of the cage. She ate rapidly, finding some satisfaction, though not the one she most desired, in sinking her yellow, over-long teeth into the flesh, and chewing it with her mouth open. Her face was wrinkled like a hag; she ate apples like an urchin. All the time she watched the Professor, but with an animal's gaze, impartially taking in his whole figure. She had not yet realised the face was the important part.

Edwina's mind was dim-lit, flitting with suspicions she was too incurious to investigate. She did not want to know the significance of the Professor's conversation with Percy, but she was jealous of it, and watched lest it camouflaged the transfer of an apple. That Percy should, this morning, reject an apple was probably subterfuge; yet if it was genuine, it was inimical to herself. Her mind had the advantage that what light entered it came through a single aperture and focused on a single object. Shrewdness, which was her substitute for intelligence, warned her. She almost knew that among the beliefs of Mankind, which Percy was catching from the Professor, was one which connected the fall of Man

24

with sex; and she dimly divined that it was in response to human standards, carried like an infection in the traffic between monkey and man, that Percy had today turned from the sour, desirable apple and left it to her to consume it all.

Watching her eat and suspect, the Professor murmured aloud, ironically:

"Comfort me with apples: for I am sick of love."

As if in prompt answer a man's voice behind him said:

"Professor Darrelhyde, I presume?"

The accent was assured; and the Professor could tell from the voice that the man was grinning.

He turned, feeling annoyed, and found himself confronting a man who was, perhaps, a few years less than thirty; well-built, though not tall; even good-looking.

The Professor would have expected from him, in this situation, some anxiety to explain himself and make it clear he was not an impertinent or, even, a pickpocket. But the young man was neither apologetic nor hurried. He stood there quite relaxed, almost casual, but alert.

He seemed self-reliant; competent. He had the appearance of a practical man, who would enjoy an electrician's work. He gave also an impression of physical courage; he had an Air Force look. The Professor associated him with some dangerous and individual sport, like sailing or climbing, in which he would depend — obviously with justification — on the neatness of both his limbs and his calculations.

He was clean. His clothes, though informal, were not those of an undergraduate; they conveyed the idea that he more usually wore a uniform or, perhaps, overalls. If his dark hair was unbrushed, it had recently been cut;

and the unshaven stubble on his chin made him look not unkempt but manly.

These were not the reasons for which the Professor usually took a dislike to men of this generation; indeed they were the very opposite: yet without good excuse, and in the midst of despising himself as illiberal, the Professor found he disliked this young man more than any he had ever seen.

"My name is Kendrick."

"I'm afraid I don't know you. Should I? You're not one of my students?"

"No. I'm in a different racket." Kendrick grinned, but the Professor was, without evidence, convinced he had no sense of humour.

The Professor ducked out from the barrier and Kendrick, without much disturbing himself, flipped his body to one side so that the Professor could emerge on to the path.

"They told me I could contact you here."

"I spend a lot of time here."

"Good enough." Kendrick laughed, perhaps remembering he had caught the Professor talking to the monkeys. "That'll be why they sent me to prepare you."

"To prepare me?"

"They thought you'd miss the beastie when he goes."

If Percy had learnt from the Professor how to be almost human, he had learnt from Percy one animal faculty. He felt neither fear nor aggression, but a general wariness of danger. He fell back a pace or two, as if better to anticipate where Kendrick was going to strike.

From this distance he could measure himself accurately. He might be middle-aged, scraggy, high-shouldered; but he was taller than Kendrick.

"What beast are you talking about?"

"What do they call him?" Kendrick glanced to the

label, and the Professor envied his strength of eyesight as he read off: "Oh — Percy."

The Professor could plumb Kendrick's full agreement with the facetious spirit which had given the animal its name. He could tell that Kendrick thought monkeys ugly and comic. He felt himself opposed by an attitude that was adamant, self-contained, cool, reasonable and irrefutable, like a legal system, but wrong.

"What do you mean, Percy is going to go? Where's he going? Who's going to take him?"

"Percy is being called to higher things."

"Called?"

"Commandeered, if you like. Liberated."

Percy was sitting at the front of the cage. Finding their conversation too difficult for him, he was staring past the two men at the sunny, holiday-like prospect of freedom.

"You don't really mean you're going to liberate him, do you?"

"No, no. It's just one of those expressions."

"It means 'scrounge'?"

"Fair enough. Scrounge, make off with."

"And who is going to make off with Percy?"

"The outfit I'm with."

The Professor paused a minute, then asked: "By whose authority does your 'outfit' propose to take Percy?" He felt his question turned to ridicule by the mock-dignity of the animal's name.

"The powers that be," Kendrick replied. "It's pretty much top priority."

"What is?"

"The whole project. Your Percy's a V.I.P."

"What do you want him for?"

"A rocket."

"You want him for a rocket?"

"To go up in a rocket."

27

A boy of eight or nine ran along the path, almost hit the Professor and then stopped, his attention caught up by the mournful aspect of the Hackenfeller's Apes. He leaned across the barrier, straining, and tried to poke a nut between the bars towards Percy. Percy turned his head away.

"This is all nonsense," the Professor said to Kendrick. "The animal belongs to the Society. Surely? I shall inform——"

"Actually, it was only loaned to the Society."

"Then it belongs to a private owner."

"It did. Our outfit bought it."

The small boy, twisting round in his position on the barrier, saw his parents come into sight and called:

"Mummy! He doesn't want a nut!"

The parents, talking themselves, paid no attention.

The Professor stared at Kendrick. "You've bought it already?"

"Absolutely. The deal's finalised."

The parents paused, lingering just near enough to the child to keep a half-attending watch over him, and the mother's glance was drawn for a second to the cage. She said to her husband, in a quiet voice the boy was not to hear:

"They don't look very happy, do they?"

"That's just their expression."

"It doesn't seem right to keep them shut up."

"They're all right," the man said. He refused to have his son's pleasure spoilt, even though his son could not hear, by any suggestion that it was unkind. "After all, there's two of them."

"Shh." She looked automatically towards the boy, lest he should have overheard a hint of how he was conceived. But he was occupied in proffering the nut. Still stretched over the barrier, he dared not go inside. Percy's sulkiness baffled and unsettled him, and he held himself ready to jerk away if the animal should prove dangerous.

"Mummy! He doesn't want a nut!"

"Save it for one that does," the woman called. She and her husband walked on.

The boy waited for a moment, offended that his parents were less curious than himself. Then, afraid of being lost in the Zoo and scared by Percy's demeanour, he dropped heavily off the barrier and ran, more nearly terrified than he had known, after his parents.

There was a deep, sunny silence, which the Professor broke into. Before he could speak, he had to clear his throat.

"Why must it be this animal in particular?"

"These are the only Hackenfeller's Apes in London."

"But why Hackenfeller's Ape, especially as it's so rare? I should have thought any of the primates——"

"That's your line. Your people said Hackenfeller's Ape would be nearest to human in its reactions."

"I suppose that would be true. What sort of reactions," he made himself ask, "do you anticipate?"

"We don't. We're sending the beastie to find out."

"Oh, of course. There will be — recording instruments, I suppose?"

"Uh-huh."

"Percy will be — strapped down?"

"He'll have some freedom of movement. Of course at some stage he'll become weightless. At certain altitudes——"

"Yes. I've read about that. What sensations go with being weightless?"

"Sensations?" Kendrick wrinkled his nose, puzzled. "You've got me there. I haven't thought, exactly. Some degree of vertigo, I suppose . . ."

The picture became clear. Percy, drunk through no debauchery of his own, reaching for walls that would not come to him; trying to sink to a floor that receded; struggling; then experiencing vertigo — some degree of vertigo; then nausea; then, at the inexplicable oddness of these sensations, which Kendrick had not thought about, panic.

"No!" the Professor exclaimed aloud.

"Something wrong?"

The wrongness of the whole idea, which was the strength of the Professor's protest, could not, he knew, be put to Kendrick. He was forced into a weaker position, on Kendrick's own ground.

"You realise I'm studying these animals?"

"You'll still have one of them."

"I'm studying their mating."

"Hah!" Kendrick was amused, probably by the Professor's earnestness. "Well, the male will be replaced in due course. Then you can take up where you left off."

"You're very impetuous about all this," the Professor said.

"I told you. It's top priority. It's top secret as well, for that matter."

"When is it to be?"

"Tuesday or Wednesday," Kendrick replied. "Probably Wednesday."

"You don't mean Tuesday or Wednesday of this week?"

"I do mean Tuesday or Wednesday of this week," Kendrick answered, smiling, relaxed, unemphatic. "There's a flap on. The met bods can't promise the right conditions after Wednesday. At the moment" — he looked up — "it's just the job."

The Professor looked up too; for the second time today he reflected that this was, indeed, perfect flying weather.

Treacherously, he asked:

"Why don't you take the female?"

"Hah! Because they're the tougher sex. She might stand up to things the male couldn't." More seriously, Kendrick added: "We might need her later if it doesn't work this time."

"You send male monkeys," the Professor said, "where male men dare not go."

Kendrick was still watching the sky, following the course of the aeroplane, just visible in the East. "Too bad, isn't it?" he agreed. "But we're all grounded. Orders from the highest level."

"You don't mean you'd be willing to go?"

"Lord love you, yes." Kendrick looked down again, and at the Professor. "I'd give my back teeth. It's just too bad." He added: "I don't see what you're worrying about. It'll be a great day for — what's his name? — Percy. Percy will see the stars."

A silence of disagreement fell between the two men, Kendrick quite at home with the idea of sending a projectile into space, and a monkey with it, treating it indeed as no more than the culmination of a thought he had tamed long ago, the Professor feeling as if, with the strange notion, he had received a draught of nothingness into his mind.

"Well," Kendrick said, looking at the watch he wore, on a steel band, on the inside of his wrist, "I must pull."

"Tuesday or Wednesday," the Professor repeated.

"Tuesday or Wednesday."

"What time?"

"Earlyish. About nine in the morning." Kendrick turned.

"How will they collect him?"

"We'll bring a van. There's no need for you to do anything. We've fixed it with the people here. It's all taped."

"If it's all fixed," — the Professor drew Kendrick back — "why did you inform me?"

Kendrick smiled with good humour. "Someone had the idea you might make trouble for us."

"I shall have to consider it."

Kendrick beamed. "Do that thing," he said affably, and strode away.

The monkeys' minds could not accommodate the new threat. Turning back, the Professor found them still absorbed in the inward reign of terror sex had imposed on them, Percy staring dolefully outwards, Edwina with her hands folded on her belly willing him to come to her.

The Zoo, already fuller, prepared for the crowd that could be expected on a hot Sunday. The attendants, the keepers of ice-cream kiosks, even the more conscious of the animals, seemed stirred by impatience to get the luncheon period over and proceed to entertain the general public in the afternoon. Carried clearly in the Sunday stillness of London, three strokes of a church bell marked the Consecration: it was near the end of a service that had begun at midday. The Professor responded by noticing he was hungry. He no longer went to church; but the habits of his childhood had left in his temperament the need to make some regular attendance on Sundays. What he did on the Sundays of his adult life was to lunch with his sister.

The plane which all morning long had seemed to be in the vicinity swooshed finally across the sky, its pilot anonymously celebrating his delight in the speed attained by Man.

The Professor approached the cage and handed Edwina the last of the apples. To Percy he offered his last exhortation:

"You've got to survive, and you've got to procreate. We may need you."

Remembering Kendrick's declaration that he might need the female monkey too, in time, the Professor hurriedly explained that he meant nothing of that sort.

"When my species has destroyed itself, we may need yours to start it all again."

He walked briskly away.

As soon as he had gone, Percy, exhausted by the attempt to understand, let his head droop; and Edwina, seeing that his energy had been wasted upon infertile purposes, moaned in fury and, still devouring the apple, set her evil and unlucky eye upon the Professor as he went.

He was full of thoughtful activities, exploring schemes. Kendrick had assumed he could make trouble: what had Kendrick had in mind? The Professor wished he had asked him, but presumably Kendrick would not have told.

Probably Kendrick expected from the Professor the usual routine of making a fuss; he supposed the Professor would stand upon what academic dignity he had, berate some of his academic subordinates and perhaps lose someone a minor job: at the end, with no good done to the monkey, the Professor would have the compensation that he had made his weight felt.

This Kendrick might expect, but the Professor was planning otherwise. He was not interested in petty methods; he had too good a case. There was enough humaneness in human kind. He had — surely? — only to appeal to it.

He passed between the flamingoes and the vultures, and left the Zoo. Out here, where the smell of the animals drained away and the ground rose, so that it was possible to feel the wind, or at least a comparative freshness, it was possible also to feel confident.

He struck across the meadow, making for the bus-stop in Albany Street. Before him lay Nash's terrace, so slim and fine that it might have been the Almaviva palace itself. A hot shimmering in the air gave the façade an ephemeral, theatrical frailty. The sky, so homogeneously blue that it might have been painted, rippled like canvas. A cloud, whorled with a light impasto, rested to the left of the pediment with precise, romantic sadness. Sunshine lay matt on all the stucco surfaces, and cast cornices and window sashes into profound relief.

He set his confidence to the tune of *Non Più Andrai.* Even in its natural tenor register his voice was crackly.

> *"Cherubino, alla vittoria*
> *Alla gloria militar!"*

He looked like a scholastic grasshopper, crossing Regents Park and shattering its pastoral calm. One or two people, also heading for Albany Street and luncheon, seemed to notice his oddity.

A clock struck and he realised that if he did not hurry he would be more than his usual fifteen minutes late. His sister was accustomed to his lateness; but after twenty years she still would not make allowance for it. She cooked the meal so that it was ready when he was due; and when, fifteen minutes afterwards, he arrived, she always warned him that if it was burned he had only himself to blame. To her, his coming late was a result of his being a man; comparable with his dreaminess, his scientificness, his impracticality and his preference for eating a roasted joint in the middle of the day even in weather like this.

He walked faster, determined to be no more than fifteen minutes late to the second. In connecting lateness with manliness his sister was probably right; but she had failed to distinguish the ruthless quality in his condition. The reason the Professor came habitually late was that he liked his meat overdone.

"Alla gloria militar!"

Monday

PERCY provoked compassion because he was imperfect. It could be left to Kendrick to admire perfect things. No doubt Kendrick would like what Rossini had made of the Countess, with her coloratura competence. Mozart's Countess was flawed — by middle-age. Perhaps it was not because he had caught him talking to the monkeys but because he had caught him being middle-aged that Kendrick made light of the Professor: it might seem to him that people aged voluntarily, through pig-headed choice. It was not so. The Professor sighed. The Countess did not want to thrust herself as she was on the Count; she did not want to alter his taste; she would have loved to give him in her person the freshness he saw in Susanna's. But she could not: and it was through this flaw that compassion made its insidious way in. It was her imperfection she lamented in notes almost too low for the soprano voice, almost de-sexed, troubling and philosophic like the notes of a bassoon.

The wonder of the world would be, to Kendrick, the fine adaptation of stuff to its function. He would think that the Countess, no longer young, ought to give up love. Kendrick liked men and machines for what they could do. The Professor liked men and monkeys for what they could not do.

It was still early and cool. Since it was a working day, the streets outside had been suddenly evacuated after the eight o'clock rush and had not yet filled up with crowds of children on what seemed everlasting holiday. Inside, the air was still fresh, full of fresh, lively sounds — the morning conversation of a hundred species.

Standing in the same place, the Professor acknowledged that it was indeed his voice which, petulant, spinsterish, defensive against Kendrick's assault, had the day before uttered the betraying words: Why don't you take the female?

Looking at Edwina now, he was shamed by her steadfastness, by the unremitting nature of her carnality, which was already fully set in train for the day.

"Ungallant," he said aloud. "Unchivalrous."

Percy snapped up the words, bewildered that new ones should appear while the old were still undigested, but perpetually willing. This pair of words he almost managed to associate with the Professor's ideal of a Man. Edwina, unconcerned with ideals, and looking for something quite unlike gallantry or chivalry from the male of her own species, kept up her glare.

Hoping to salve himself with Edwina and so to have an untwisted conscience behind him in the day's efforts, the Professor took an apple from his pocket. Before he could present it, Edwina's arm struck between the bars. She grabbed the apple, and vaunted her quickness over Percy.

The Professor had come partly through habit and partly to give the animals a report on his progress. So far, however, it was more an apology he had to give. He had made a false start. He assured them, and himself, he would do better today.

He had taken the problem to his sister, knowing her to have been resourceful in a hundred hard cases. Moreover, as a romantic, he had it in his nature to admire all women as he admired Susanna and the Countess, and to perceive compassion and tenderness in them all.

He had not been totally mistaken, but in his sister compassion burned fiercer than he had supposed.

As he told the story, she interrupted:

"Do eat up, Clem. Goodness knows you were late enough to start with."

He thought her sympathy was even prompter than he had credited and had jumped ahead of his tale to the right conclusion. Finishing, he expected to find her full of practical suggestions. Instead, she sighed.

"Honestly, Clem, I can't make you out. All this for a monkey!"

"I——"

"Don't you know," she asked, earnestly leaning across the table, "that people human beings, Clem — are starving in India; that men are dying in Malaya; that we still haven't cured cancer; that poor old women are sent to prison for a year for stealing a cake of soap; that we still practise the barbaric rite of Capital Punishment——"

"All this is true," he began.

"It's fact. You ought to face it."

"I admit these are wrongs——"

"Wrongs, and shameful injustices."

"But the fact," he concluded, "that these are bigger wrongs and injustices doesn't make it right or just to sacrifice an innocent monkey. It doesn't alter the case at all."

"It doesn't alter the case. It alters you."

"That's absurd," he said.

"It doesn't make the case right but it makes you wrong. Honestly, I think you must be a frivolous sort of person. Here you are with all your brain — far more than I ever had — and all this needing to be done in the world, and you spend your time and energy on an animal!"

He did not see why fighting for Percy should provoke the charge that he was uncharitable towards everyone else.

"Surely you can see," she went on, " —— you, with your clear mind! — that if the rocket has to go up, it's far better to send the monkey than let some young man go risking his life."

"Ah, wait a minute!" the Professor cried. "That's it! There's the sin of it! The monkey has no choice. If Kendrick went, he'd be risking his own life, of his own free will."

"And they were quite right to stop him," she replied. "Whoever forbade it was very wise. I dare say there are plenty of foolhardy young men who ought to be doing a serious job of work for Mankind, here on the ground, who would be only too pleased to go up in a rocket just to see what it felt like to travel through space."

He protested wryly: "That's my point. If men get giddy, or whatever you do get, they know it's because they're travelling in space. If they feel themselves dropping unconscious, they know it's because of lack of pressure, or oxygen, or whatever it is. But the onkey doesn't know what it's all about."

His protest died away as he saw her purse her lips.

"I don't see why we're arguing," she said. "You admit the monkey won't know what's happening to it. pressure, or oxygen, or whatever it is. But the monkey than a human being."

The Professor had been, not fairly, he thought, but decisively, beaten: and now Percy, as if he had known in what low esteem the Professor's sister held him, let his broad, sorrowful head fall forward, and huddled himself away, immobile, looking like a memorial, put up by the defeated side, to yesterday's engagement.

Edwina's stillness seemed more alive, the stillness of implacable hope. She was, of the two, the more animated, the more animal, the less attractive. Smaller, she had proved what Kendrick had prophesied: tougher. She had forgotten Africa and freedom. Adapted not only to being a monkey but to being a caged monkey, she could, if Percy had concurred, have made their cage into a comfortable marital domain.

If the Professor had himself been a monkey, her animality might have attracted him. As it was, he was impervious to her, and she could take no comfort from him.

He put his hand, thoughtlessly, into his pocket. Edwina sprang forward, demanding another apple, her eyes flashing white as she dared Percy to get there first.

Beyond doubt, Edwina was shrewish.

He could not escape the thought that it was Percy who had made her so, and all Percy's progress was by way of Edwina's shoulders, thrusting her down. He was almost glad to accuse the monkey, since that would make it less bitter if he was to be lost; but even as he looked at him with accusation he found that Percy had forestalled him and had turned his sweet, clownish face, expressive of deep emotion and elementary thought, upon Edwina, full of sorrow for her shrewishness and guilt because he was its cause.

How long, even if Kendrick had not interfered, could Percy hold out? On the one side, Edwina's demands; on the other his self-erosion. How soon would he ease his conscience towards her by yielding to her, only to find he had a bad conscience towards his ideals? How long before he succumbed to whatever mindless state it might be that overtook a monkey that had gone mad?

A mad monkey. In the moment's image, the Professor understood Percy's dilemma. Percy was in love. It was not lack of desire, but desire too strong, too prickly, too fantastic. What the animal yearned after, when he gazed forlornly out of his cage, was the freedom to make love to Edwina of his own choice, to

40

persuade and implore her; to aspire and range; to break into that domain which, in fact, he could not break out of.

"Why," the Professor said, "Percy is a romantic, too."

Edwina cared nothing for it. Lacking foresight, she could not imagine letting Percy go in order that he might come back. If the bars of the cage had been miraculously loosed, she would have resented Percy's stepping outside. Even, the Professor thought, if she had been able to envisage Percy's fate at the hands of Kendrick, she would have spent the last moments clamouring for her due before he left.

Percy opposed to this his idealistic obstinacy. If he could not be free, he could not, or would not, be fertile.

He sighed, humanly.

It appeared that a newspaper office was the last place where one ought to come to see a journalist. The Professor told several people what he wanted, and then was shewn into an office where, he was promised, a reporter would come to attend to him.

There were three desks, jammed close together, each with a typewriter. From time to time a man or a woman looked round the door. One or two came in and searched for something in the drawers of the desks. They greeted the Professor, without asking who he was, and went away.

At last a reporter arrived, a man of thirty or more, trained to efface himself for the purposes of his job.

"Sorry to have kept you. You must be getting hungry."

The Professor was surprised: but he looked at his watch and found it was indeed past lunch-time.

He began to explain:

41

"I thought if you could launch a campaign — you see, I'm sure the public will feel strongly about this, if only they can be told the facts. These people act in such a hole-and-corner way. They only told me yesterday. I'm afraid you'll be rather rushed?"

"Everything in journalism is a rush. It's an occupational risk."

"Then you'll know how to cope with it."

"Don't worry about that."

"I feel it will succeed, you know."

The reporter nodded. "We'd better get cracking. Let's straighten out the facts, for a start. This animal's name — Percy, you said?"

"Percy. Yes."

"That's rather a good angle, you know. In this job we're always looking for what we call angles. And your name?"

It relaxed him not to have to plead his case; apparently it would be elicited from him. The reporter would not argue back; the Professor would not have to make himself appear a sentimentalist.

He felt serene in entrusting Percy's safety to this young man's competence in presenting angles.

"You're a professor?"

"Yes."

"Of zoology?"

"Yes."

"By the way, is Percy a monkey or an ape?"

"There's no difference."

"Oh? I had an idea an ape was more advanced, or something?"

"Most people have." The Professor smiled, in friendship, at the young man. "I think it must have been invented by a newspaper like yours."

"Pity. Would have made a good angle. Now. Who's sending up this rocket?"

"I'm afraid I don't really know."

"No clues?"

"I know it's top priority, and top secret."

"Oh. Government stuff. Defence."

"I suppose so."

The reporter closed his book, and stood up.

"What's the matter?"

"We can't use it."

"Why not? Because it's secret?"

"No, that side's been quite easy since the war."

"Then what is it?"

"I don't know," the reporter said, "if you ever read our paper?"

"I'm afraid——"

"I don't altogether blame you. Anyway, if you'd seen our leaders over the past six months, you'd know what I mean. We've been pressing on with defence. Don't relax, and that sort of thing. The price of liberty is eternal vigilance."

"You couldn't go against that?"

"Oh, no. It's policy."

"I should have thought," Darrelhyde said, "that sending up rockets was offence rather than defence."

The reporter shook his head. "Everything to do with war is called defence nowadays. I think it's an American word."

"Then you won't print anything at all?"

"No. In any case, now I come to think of it, we can't discourage space travel. We run a space corner every Saturday."

"Do you?"

"For the kids. It does them less harm than sadistic comics."

It took the Professor a moment to abandon hope; another moment to see that he was meant to leave.

"I'm afraid I've taken up a lot of your time. For nothing."

"That's all right. Half this job consists of writing things that never get into print."

No longer concerned with his job, the reporter became a personality. The Professor was encouraged.

"I wonder if you would do one last thing for me?"

"What's that?"

"You always have the weather reports here, don't you? I wonder if you'd find out for me what it will be like tomorrow, and the day after."

"I think I might." He spoke into the telephone. "Give me Jill, would you?"

Waiting, he looked at the Professor over the receiver. "Got something on?"

"I just wondered if the hot spell might break."

"I shouldn't——" The phone crackled. "Hullo? Weather forecast, please, Jill."

The machine talked for a minute, inaudibly to the Professor, and he waited till the reporter put down the receiver.

"I'll spare you the details. The general impression seems to be Set Fair."

He took the Professor to the door, and apparently felt an impulse of kindliness. He put his hand on the Professor's shoulder. "Don't look so down. It's harder to burst into print than you'd think. Anyway, you'll have good weather for your picnic."

"It will be no picnic," the Professor said. He knew he had made a joke, but for all his good will towards the young man he could not smile.

He felt as he sat in the bus that a truce had been called. He had, when he left the newspaper office, made another appointment, ringing up from a public box:

44

but that was for four o'clock. Meanwhile he seemed to be a party to one of those truces called in the ancient world in order that both sides might gather up their dead.

He passed a vegetarian restaurant. Even so late as this, it was full. Through its window he could see a party of Indians at one table and next to them a party of white people. The Indians did not interest him. Probably they abstained from flesh because they seriously believed, as the Professor could not consider believing, in metempsychosis. The Europeans had no such traditional religion. They seemed to him cranks, but noble cranks: they set out to be more gentle than Jesus himself. If they had been present, the Professor wondered, at the miracle of the Loaves and Fishes, would they have accepted the bread and refused their share of the fish?

He left the bus and went into the Corner House where he knew he could still get a hot meal. It turned out to be a rissole of hashed meat. His knowledge of comparative anatomy was no use; the meat had gone through a mincing machine and he could not identify it. It seemed to him a macabre reflexion that a human body was so sacred that soldiers would break off in the middle of war to collect it and give it a solemn burial, whereas an animal's body could be mangled past recognition and still not offend the human appetite.

Once more he was kept waiting, this time in the large, polished office of the Co-ordinator of Scientific Studies, a man named Post.

The journey to Bloomsbury had proved complex: and the Professor was irritated to find all his activities slow and impeded in comparison with the plans he had made for them. Moving through immediacy and the world of affairs, both of which it was his habit to avoid, he found them denser substances than he had thought.

Post hurried in, and though he carried a bundle of paper files he looked rather a business man than a scholar.

"I'm sorry to have kept you. Look here, give me just a minute more, will you?" The request seemed framed to flatter Darrelhyde: how could Darrelhyde refuse him a minute more? "If I don't put these away now I'll never find them again."

Post was unique in these surroundings because he did not use a university accent. He spoke a mild cockney which Darrelhyde had for long thought Australian: but a reference of Post's to his childhood had revealed it as the accent of Southend and had, for a reason Darrelhyde did not stop to analyse, made Darrelhyde like him better. He seemed to stick to his accent as a badge that he was indeed different in kind from the scholars he worked with. A big, bulging man, he wore a business man's blue suit, whose pinstripes appeared to distort themselves out of true in order to cover his belly. Expert in none of the sciences, he collected and organised scientists. Perhaps they felt some contempt flowing towards them, as academics, from the man of affairs: they retaliated by saying Post was self-educated. Darrelhyde, differing from his colleagues by liking the man, differed also by regarding self-education as the only true education. If he found fault with Post's thinking, it was because Post trusted himself too little and the printed word of his teachers too much: Darrelhyde pictured him owning and studying whole shelves-ful of digests and popular educators.

"Right." Post drew his chair to the desk. "I wish I'd never heard of these summer schools and evening classes. Then I could keep my vacations to myself the way you do."

A touch of the scholar's fear of contempt made Darrelhyde say: "I've been doing some work of my own, you know, this vacation."

"So you have. So you have." Post's eyes indicated that he was referring mentally to some schedule on which — perhaps with coloured flags? — he mapped the activities of his charges. "You've been observing this monkey, haven't you?"

"Yes," Darrelhyde said. "But if you don't do something to help, the monkey will be whisked from under my nose."

"Frankly, I don't see what I can do."

"You've no influence with the Zoo?"

"It doesn't rest with the Zoo. It rests with the private owner."

"You know about this, then?" Darrelhyde asked. "From another source?"

"Just one of the threads I keep my overworked fingers on. We have some people doing rocket research."

"Then you could give me the private owner's name?"

"He's sold the monkey."

"He might reconsider."

"He's abroad, anyhow."

"Where?"

"Africa."

"Give me his address, and I'll cable. I'm prepared to spend money on this."

"I haven't got his address."

"His bank would know."

"I understand he's up country somewhere. He's inaccessible."

"Why? What's he doing there? He's not——"

"Yes, he's getting more animals, I believe. They fetch a good price at the moment."

Darrelhyde was angry. "I suppose the more rockets they send up the better price they get for the victims."

"My dear fellow," Post began. "I had no idea you took it so seriously. But you must adapt yourself to life. You must accept things."

"Accept what things?"

Post shrugged. "You should know. The oldest adage in natural history — nature red in tooth and claw."

Darrelhyde did not answer.

"Correct me if I'm wrong," Post continued, "but isn't that how Evolution works? The strong exploiting the weak all the way up the line?"

The Professor examined himself. His Evolutionary belief had itself been evolving in these last months. It no longer seemed to him that Evolution proceeded by strengthening the strong: rather it used as its vessel the weak and inadequate, as though they possessed some special felicity that was more fertile than strength.

He said: "Possibly Man rose by exploiting the weak. If you study his fossil record there's blood in his footprints. That's how he came up. But now — now, he is up. The very thing that marks his up-ness is that he knows better."

"You believe," Post asked, "the world is improving?"

Darrelhyde was suspicious. "You're going to tell me that wars are getting bigger and bloodier."

"I wasn't, actually. I was going to ask if you think we're kinder to animals than our ancestors were."

"Well of course we are! You've only to walk round London. The place is full of societies for preserving them and healing them and so forth."

Post concentrated and frowned; and Darrelhyde had for the first time the impression that he was laying aside the influence of his home educators, and that his words now were the record of a battle he had fought for himself. "Cavemen," he said solemnly, "used to hunt animals when the animals came their way. They ran a fair risk of being killed by the animals. We on the other hand rear animals, we selectively, and if need be forcibly, breed them, and fatten them: all with no purpose in mind except to kill them in the prime of life or even sooner."

"At least," Darrelhyde said, "we kill them humanely now."

"If someone had offered to bump you off at thirty, would you have been reconciled to him on condition he did it humanely?"

Post had spoken with surprising animus: and Darrelhyde murmured: "You ought to be a vegetarian."

"Those people make me sick!" Post retorted.

"You think they're sentimental?"

"I think they delude themselves. Don't they realise that if they eat lettuce the lettuce-grower will shoot the rabbits who maraud the lettuces? If they drink milk the farmer will slaughter the bull calf who can't yield the stuff. Vegetarians indeed! They can't get out of it as easily as that."

"Ah," Darrelhyde said, "you're talking about Original Sin."

"No, about the Origin of Species."

"The mark of Cain, then."

"The mark of Cain," Post agreed, "that can't be erased. All the consciousness of Man only goes to shew him the mark is there — it doesn't remove it."

"It's not the consciousness of Man that distinguishes him," Darrelhyde protested; "it's his imagination. If you can imagine what it feels like to be an animal, and you must kill it, then you kill it humanely." He added: "If you can imagine what it feels like to be a middle-aged Countess, then you write an opera."

"If you must kill it!" Post mocked. "Why *must* you kill animals? You know as well as I do that Man can live perfectly healthily on a vegetable diet. Everyone knows. But we still say it's necessary to kill animals. The figures shew that you can stop hanging murderers without encouraging murder, but we go on behaving as if hanging was necessary. The last two wars brought economic ruin to Europe but we still think that war is an economic necessity."

"We made a mistake."

"Mistake nothing! Mankind invents necessities right and left to justify what it enjoys doing. And let me tell you that all the periods when your operas and other forms of art have flourished have been characterised by the most bloodthirsty 'necessities'. The Greeks believed slavery was necessary to stable government. The Victorians believed empire was necessary to progress. The more consciousness any culture has, the more it enjoys cruelty. That," Post cried, "is what the consciousness of Man amounts to! That's what his imagination is! I don't suppose a tiger much enjoys tearing up its prey. It just does it. And it can't imagine what the prey feels like. The distinguishing mark of Man is that he can, and he enjoys it!"

"You think war is something men want?"

"Well, it's a human activity. I presume it's caused by men not pixies."

Darrelhyde smiled. "We ought to hand the world over to women. They lack these aggressive instincts."

"Ah, romantic!" Post said sourly.

"I know."

"Women could have stopped war long ago by the boycott system. They could have refused to go to bed with the soldiers."

"Like the *Lysistrata*."

Not understanding the reference, Post ignored it. "But in fact," he went on, "after every great war, when all the men are soldiers, the birth-rate rises. And the symbols that stand for fertility in dreams — women's dreams as well as men's — are swords and guns."

"Then we're all fundamentally cruel? We always have been?"

"Let me tell you what I've worked out," Post said. "You'll agree the basic situation is the child's — loves his mother, hates his father?"

"The Oedipus situation."

"A two-edged situation," Post said. "Love and hate. Art and empire. Well, this Oedipus situation has had various offspring at various times. First there was the question of incest. A strong repugnance for it, coupled with a strong unconscious desire to commit it. At the time of Byron and Shelley, incest was the thrill of the day."

"It was still a live issue," Darrelhyde put in, "when Bernard Shaw began writing plays."

Post ignored that, too, and continued: "Well, I daresay as much incest goes on now as ever it did. But it's only reported in the Sunday papers. It isn't a question of the moment any more. It was pushed out by the Oscar Wilde trial."

Darrelhyde agreed. "Gide. Proust. The age of the Baron de Charlus."

"But even that," Post said, "has gone now. Of course some people still think it's fashionable. But they're not important now. They're out of date."

"They're still persecuted," Darrelhyde said.

"Persecuted?"

"The law——"

"Oh, the law, yes. The law's even more out of date. It always is. It still puts people in prison for incest, too. But I tell you that's just Sunday paper stuff. It doesn't matter *socially*. No one's shocked any more. You never hear of anyone refusing to have a homosexual to tea, do you?"

Darrelhyde tried to remember. "When did tolerance come in? With the twenties, I suppose."

"After the Great War. And you know why. Because the Great War began yet another age: the one we're living in now."

Darrelhyde slowly asked: "The Age of Cain?"

"The Age of Cain. I dare say there's no more cruelty now than there used to be. But it's not natural any more. It's not unthinking cruelty; it's neurotic cruelty. War goes on for the same old excuses, but it's suddenly become a problem. If you'd spoken to Sir Francis Drake, who was a buccaneering old slave-trader, about the problem of war, he wouldn't have known what you meant. I dare say" — Post spread his hands — "there's no more crime than there used to be. But everyone's suddenly thinking about it, and reading detective stories and tough American thrillers and other forms of mild pornography. And the papers are full of letters from people who imagine themselves to be decent peaceable citizens, demanding harsher measures against the criminal. And letters from humanitarian reformers saying all the Judges ought to be hanged."

"So I'm living in the Age of Cain," Darrelhyde concluded. "I always did feel a repugnance towards the twentieth century." He stood up. "Well. What shall we do about it?"

"Do? What can one do? Man will always invent a new necessity for what he enjoys."

"Don't be so gloomy. We get round bits of necessity from time to time. We know now that slavery isn't necessary. Perhaps we shall find war isn't."

"Oh, I quite agree," said Post, to the Professor's surprise. "War will become impossible very soon."

"There you are! The very terror of the weapons will defeat their own end. I tell you, sadism can be harnessed. I suppose surgeons are basically sadistic men, but it's turned to good account. And now, if the war weapons get more and more fearful——"

"More and more rockets going up," Post reminded him.

Darrelhyde paused. "If I could be sure," he said finally, "that Percy's death would help make war impossible——"

"Oh, it will. War will soon be as unthinkable as hunting for one's food."

Darrelhyde could see the trap prepared. "Well?"

"You know what has replaced hunting one's food — the abattoir."

"Well?"

"Perhaps you've noticed that open war is already being replaced by the concentration camp and the extermination chamber."

"I take back what I said about Percy."

Post stood up, dismissively. "My dear chap, there really is nothing you can do except adapt yourself to the facts of life."

"Advocatus Diaboli."

"You really are too cultured for me. Was that the Latin name for Hackenfeller's Ape?"

"You won't do anything, then?"

"Beyond advising you to relax, what can I do? You'll give yourself a nervous breakdown if you go on like this."

Darrelhyde opened the door, remembering his fear that Percy might go mad.

It was unusual for the Professor's sister to telephone him on a Monday, because on Mondays she had always seen him only the day before.

The phone rang while he was in the bath, hunched up, trying to clean his feet after his field work in the habitat of Mankind. He left it to his landlady to answer; but presently she called, contralto, down the corridor:

"Professor Darrelhyde! It's for you!"

"I'm in the bath. Do you know who it is?"

"She says she's your sister."

He pulled himself up, angrily, and almost slipped. He had an idea his landlady thought she was scoring with her hint of disbelief: — She *says* she's your sister. She and the other old women who lived in the house were evidently now hiding, as if they expected him to come out of the bathroom without remembering to put on his dressing-gown.

He hurried to the phone.

"Oh, Clem? I have a feeling I wasn't very kind to you yesterday."

"Hum."

"You're not taking it very graciously."

"I'm sorry. But it's not a question of being kind or otherwise. It's a question of principle."

"I thought it was all about the principle of being kind."

"Perhaps you're right. I'm too tired to argue."

"Clem, dear, you don't sound very well."

"I'm perfectly all right."

"I suppose you've been thinking about that blessed monkey all day?"

"I haven't been just thinking. I've been acting."

"What have you fixed up?"

"Nothing."

"You sound what's called peevish and overwrought. Have you taken your temperature?"

"I'm all right."

"Would you like to come over here where I can look after you?"

"I'm just going to bed. I was in the bath when you rang."

"You mustn't get a chill, then. Would you like me to come to you?"

"It would be better if you didn't. There's some disbelief here that you are in fact my sister."

"What did you say, Clem?"

"Nothing. An irrelevancy."

"You sound distraught to me. They would have the telephone in the corridor where you're bound to catch cold. Clem, why do you go on living in that awful place?"

He made no reply.

"You could afford something nicer, couldn't you?"

"I suppose I can't be bothered to change."

"Oh, dear," she said. "Men."

"I think you and I bring out the worst in each other. I think I'll go back to my bath."

"You're sure you don't want me? I could be there in half an hour. I could bring some extra blankets."

He asked sardonically: "All this for a man?"

He felt the old women were spying on him on his way back to the bathroom.

The bath had grown cool. He ran in more hot water, against the rules of the house, and watched his narrow, unsightly body grow pink and puckered.

He was possessed, suddenly, by a deep, subversive chuckling. It appeared to be the revolt of a mind that would support no more attacks, marking the vigour of his disagreement with Post: it was also the revolt of the romantic admirer of women. This was something anti-romantic; robust; even coarse. He took the cake of soap out of the soap-dish on the side of the bath, and deliberately incised with his thumbnail a crude, unpleasant drawing.

He replaced the soap; then lay back, filled with boiling, anticipatory laughter. It was his hope that one of the old women, coming after him to take a bath, would idly pick up the soap; and then glance down at it; and then — this seemed almost too much richness to expect — scream.

Tuesday

He was late arriving: for two reasons. He had waited till the bank opened, and drawn out some money. Secondly, he had been restrained by a cowardly, backward half-hope. Kendrick had named this or the next day; he had said he would come early; he had said the experiment was urgent. Perhaps when the Professor arrived he would find it was all over already.

He passed between the vultures and the flamingoes, creatures no less extravagant and bizarre than Man, as though between two fantastically ornamental gateposts, leading to a palatial labyrinth. On the floor beneath the vultures' perches lay nuggets of still bleeding meat, the remains of some small mammal.

He descended the slope and went through the shady, echoing tunnel. Coming in sight of the monkeys' cage, he at once made out the bulk of two figures, back turned to back, irreconcilable.

Percy was still here; but this might be his last morning. It was clear and still faintly dewy, promising miles and miles of visibility.

Where were Percy's thoughts? Was he wandering in whatever conception he might have of a Forest of Arden, attaching love verses to the trees? Or was he already in the flare-lit, grotto-ornamented, statue-sprinkled garden of Count Almaviva, masked, wooing the wrong woman in the dark, keeping assignations, speaking asides; entangled in the symmetrical pattern of formal comedy and all the imbroglios of plot which beset and postponed the marriage of Susanna to her Figaro, just as, for different reasons, the marriage had been postponed between Percy and Edwina?

It was nonsense. Percy's thoughts were enclosed by the cage, and he was no freer in his imagination than in his body. And alas, good beast, the dénouement which waited for him was far from formal.

Perhaps if he had been able to guess what Kendrick proposed, Percy would have thought it no worse a tragedy than the puzzle he had been confronting all these weeks: why was he imprisoned, and why, being imprisoned, could he not console himself by taking what he most desired?

Edwina was equally unable to share the Professor's feeling that time was running out in Kendrick's favour. For weeks now all time had been stealing sweetness from her. All moments were filched from the brief period when she was capable of conceiving.

Unable to apprehend the future, Percy had no memory worth the name and, though some human beings had become familiar to him, he had small means of distinguishing one from the next. When he could recall so little of Africa itself, how was he to recall which particular human being had, in Africa, lured him into a trap, or which had put him in a cage in London for ever after? Darrelhyde realised that Percy held him, Darrelhyde, responsible for his captivity. The idea horrified him; he hastened to disclaim it; but Percy did not understand and continued to appeal to the man whom he saw as omnipotent and all-responsible.

He was trustful, and without bitterness. He did not find it incongruous that the Professor, having captured him, should pity his captivity; nor that the man who had, as he thought, put him in it, should urge him by some means he could not grasp to transcend his cage.

Darrelhyde could not tell whether Percy's acceptance was the perfection of humility or whether it meant, as Advocatus Diaboli would maintain, that Percy was tinged with doom and invited murder.

It was time to go. He had an appointment with a Colonel Hunter whose name he had found in the telephone book.

The mid-morning crowd was swelling round him.

On the way out, he met the youth whose job it was to sweep Percy's cage. He was newly appointed; his hair was too long; instead of working he struck attitudes with his broom. Darrelhyde thought him a lout.

"Morning, Professor. Nothing happening yet?"

The lout did not know that the comic opera had become melodramatic, and the suspense had moved on from the question of consummating Percy's marriage to the question of keeping him on the earth.

"Nothing yet."

"Too bad."

Neither did he know that the Professor was moving after his quarry, his wallet fat against his chest with fifty pound notes, as he prepared to beat the world of affairs, by every weapon at the command of a citizen, into giving him back Percy's life.

The Colonel's office was in a side street near Leicester Square. It was not easy to find. The Professor wandered for a minute or two in a neighbourhood which smelt, to his nostrils, of depravity. There was nothing explicit. Figures loitered and figures flitted. The details were undivinable, but the general trend was plain. He reflected that Edwina was not alone, and not purely bestial, in being able to stomach such suggestions before lunch.

A sign caught his attention. It was made of metal,

three or four feet deep. Haphazard floating strips of wire and a few grimy light bulbs added an effect of medieval illumination to each letter, and shewed that the whole sign had once been capable of being illuminated in the modern sense. It was placed high up, and dominated the blank wall of a building on the far side of the street: a multi-storied place, gothic in intent, made of dirty red-brown brick. Just above the level of the first floor a course of green and white tiles had been let into the façade.

It was not what he had expected, but not even his eye-sight could mistake the sign.

LEAGUE FOR THE PREVENTION OF
UNKIND PRACTICES TO ANIMALS

He crossed the road, passing a small restaurant whose plate-glass window was obscured by net curtains; they were draped back only in the centre — to display, where one might have expected a woman's hat, a cold ham. He passed on to find the front door of the building.

There was a lofty entrance hall, dark and indifferently clean, partly tiled in imitation of marble. Beyond that, a pair of swing doors of later date, made of glass, chromium and a startling yellow wood, admitted him to a shabby foyer, lit by a pale blue strip on the ceiling. In the middle was an occasional table piled with glossy magazines unfamiliar to the Professor, all of them creased. Opposite him was a desk.

With the girl who sat behind it the Professor was for a moment at cross purposes, until he established that, despite the sign, only a small portion of the building was connected with Colonel Hunter. The girl indeed had never heard of him, but she directed the Professor to look at the list in the lobby. It took him a second to follow her meaning; then he pushed through the swing doors again and found the list on his left in the hall. It stood almost the full height of the wall, engraved in brass like a memorial tablet. The occupants of the ground floor were listed lowest, then the others in ascending order through the building. Standing on his toes, the Professor could just make out, above his head:

> 5th floor: League for the Prevention of
> Unkind Practices to Animals
> Col. Hunter

When he returned, the girl was with a man who had long hair and fat hips.

"Did you find it?" the girl asked.

"Yes, thank you. It's on the fifth floor. Could you please tell me where to find the stairs?"

"There."

They were just to the right, obvious.

"Oh, of course. I'm sorry to have put you to so much trouble. It was just a mistake. I see from the list that you're a theatrical agency."

"That's right."

"Not at all what I was looking for." The Professor made towards the stairs; but the fat man said:

"Take some literature with you."

"Oh no, thank you. I'm not an impresario."

"That's all right. It's free. It'll be something to read on the way up."

As soon as the staircase took a turn that brought it out of sight from the foyer, the carpet ceased and the concrete steps became deeper and their incline sharper. The walls were painted olive green, and splintered. Little pits in their surface made Darrelhyde think of his childhood, because they revealed a colourless graininess, like the inside of a clay marble. Here and there, in dusky angles on his route, a dry cigarette-end lay where it had been cast.

He passed several landings and at last reached a dingy door of frosted glass, with the Colonel's name on it. He waited for a moment outside, to pant, and glanced at the paper the fat man had given him. It shewed, in blunt line drawing, a chimpanzee wearing knickers and riding a bicycle. "This act can be booked through the West End Theatrical and Variety . . ." He threw it down the stairwell before knocking at the door.

The Colonel was a tall, broad-shouldered man in good condition, with a very big, red, plain face. He greeted the Professor—

"Darrelhyde, my dear chap!"
as though they were friends, and the volume of his voice made the Professor question how the girl five stories below could have remained ignorant of him.

He drew the Professor in, to a tiny room which made no pretence of being more than an office. It had a bare floor and green filing cabinets along the walls. Being high up, it was light. There were no curtains. Hunter sat down in a round-shouldered swivel chair, and the Professor faced him, over his desk, sitting on a kitchen chair.

"You told me a certain amount on the phone. Would you care to enlarge on that?"

"Perhaps I may start," the Professor said, "by saying I am, of course, prepared to pay for any help you may give."

"I won't pretend I'm sorry to hear it. Heaven knows, I'd like to do this for nothing. But it's no good beating about the bush, is it? Incidentally, since this is rather urgent, could you pay us in cash? Always provided," the Colonel added, louder than ever, smiling, his eyes honest and blue, "we can fix you up?"

"Yes, I've thought of that."

"Good man. Well, now."

Evidently it was for the Professor to lead. "Can you help me?" he said.

"What had you in mind?" The Colonel leaned back, and crooked his knee against the desk.

"I wondered if you — being in this milieu, as it were, which is entirely strange to me — had any acquaintances among the authorities."

"Ah, the authorities. No. I'm afraid not. Not those authorities."

"No. I suppose the police are no help?"

"Seldom," said Hunter. "In fact, the balance of our experience goes to shew that it is best not to drag them in."

"You haven't any pull with influential people?"

"Pull," Hunter repeated. "Now by 'pull', Professor, you mean blackmail. Don't deny it. Well, I can tell you, this organisation has nothing whatever to do with blackmail."

"It looks as if we shall have to use public agitation," Darrelhyde said.

"Ah. Of what kind?"

"Isn't there something called lobbying M.P.s?"

"Sending a monkey up in a rocket, you know, doesn't infringe any law. In fact, the existing laws don't allow for rockets. Rockets are a new departure."

"Yes."

"Departure," the Colonel emphasised, and laughed at his joke.

"Well, what about protest meetings? Petitions? Pickets in Downing Street?"

"Now you're moving into the paths of notoriety."

"And you won't follow me there?"

"This organisation," the Colonel enunciated, "has found it more profitable to avoid the paths of notoriety."

He smiled in a way which, in the middle-aged man, was boyish. In a boy it would have been sinister. "The better part of valour is discretion."

The Professor asked himself what Colonel Hunter's voice could have to do with discretion. "What you mean," he said, "is that you can't help me."

The Colonel made no direct answer. "I'm very glad you brought the case to us. There are some terrible things going on in this world. Terrible indeed." He opened a drawer in his desk and took out a bundle of photographs. "Look at those."

It was many years since the Professor had done any dissecting, yet, looking back, he was sure that not even in his greenest student years had he felt this nausea. In the laboratory there had always been the sharp, continual interest of intellectual discovery, which had taken off from disgust; rather as, he had argued, Kendrick's intellectual curiosity would have allayed the terror of going up in the rocket. Here, however, there was no intellectual content. The background had been painted out to focus the attention. Moreover, it seemed to him that the photographs were carefully graded in horror through the bundle, with the most horrifying at the end.

"I'll shew you something else," Hunter said. "A real prize."

He brought out a key-ring and, suddenly grown jerky, fiddled to select the right key. He bent down and unlocked the door of a small cabinet next to his desk. "It's one of Pavlov's original dogs," he whispered. "A classic."

Leaving the door ajar, he motioned to the Professor.

The Professor bent down beside the cabinet and, closing his eyes, pretended to look in.

"I had to pay a pretty price to get that stuffed and smuggled out," the Colonel said.

Darrelhyde stood up. "You can't help me."

63

"Perhaps I can't. But — it's always better to be frank — *you* could help *me*."

"I doubt it."

"You haven't even asked me how. You can't know if you can or not."

"Very well, then. How?"

"Why beat about the bush? You could become a member of the League."

"What good would that do me?"

"We'd send you photographs regularly, every time we got a new batch. We have some good sources of supply."

"No, thank you."

"Well, don't you think you ought to do it for the good of your soul?" the Colonel said. "Your Charley isn't the only monkey on the beach. What about doing something for the animal kingdom in general?"

"How would my joining help that?"

"By bringing abuses to the public notice."

"How?"

"By the wider dissemination," the Colonel said, "of pictures like these."

The Professor was looking straight into the Colonel's eyes, but he could not be sure if the Colonel twinkled, almost winked.

"Goodbye."

"Wait a minute, wait a minute!"

The Colonel bent down beside the cabinet and looked for a moment inside. Then he locked the door, put away his keys, and rose, puffed but with refreshed geniality.

"My good Professor, I can't let you go in this inconsolable frame of mind. I like to send people away looking on the brighter side."

"Do you have many successes?" the Professor asked.

"Come, come, don't be bitter. I bear you no ill will,

even if you won't join our crusade. In fact, I think that's quite understandable from a scientist like yourself. One expects scientists to be cruel in order to be kind."

"None of this helps my monkey. His name is Percy incidentally."

"Percy, then. What I want you to realise is that your Percy is being sacrificed in a good cause."

"I'd rather he wasn't sacrificed at all."

"Naturally, naturally. But since it must be, think of the good that will come of it."

"What good?"

"Do you know what all these rockets are leading to? Space stations! Great platforms miles above the earth. Apparently, once you get the things out there they just go on circling round and round."

"I know that," the Professor said, walking to the door. "It doesn't help."

"Of course it helps! Use your imagination! How can people be kind to animals," Hunter roundly asked, "while they're worried to distraction about another war? But just let us have a couple of space stations up there, and you'll find these Ruskies aren't half so cock-a-hoop. I know the Ruskie. What he respects is strength. When he knows we're up there, like the eye of God, seeing everything he does, with his industrial areas and his centres of population wide open to us —by jove," he finished, "we'll be able to bomb hell out of the Ruskies."

"I don't think," the Professor said, "Percy would want to die for that."

He had descended one flight when he heard Colonel Hunter's enormous footsteps clanging behind him.

"I say!"

"Yes?"

"If you could get any photographs when that rocket comes down——"

"Photographs of the rocket?"

65

"Of the rocket and its occupant. We could pay."

"I doubt if it will come down in one piece," said Darrelhyde.

"That," said Colonel Hunter, "would be even better."

The unrestrained light of afternoon flooded the Park. Now at its most mature, its roundest and most fruitful, it was like a peony all but overblown, pregnant to bursting point, the hard seeds audible inside the plump seed cases. At any moment the rich day would break into dusk.

All round the Zoo, although the sunshine looked fit to last for ever, children and toys were being collected and waste paper was being thrown away.

The Professor had come as reluctantly as a man going to a funeral. He felt it his duty to take some sort of farewell, or at least to come and mourn.

The animals were not aware of any need for farewells. Edwina was relentlessly and rhythmically playing her own tune of malevolent desire. Percy was close up against the bars in his favourite position, clinging there by the power of one brutal, hairy arm. Infinitely stronger than his mentor in everything except intellect, he looked to the Professor with the trust of a simpleton.

Neither animal took any notice of the crowds. They were used to Mankind which, arriving full of curiosity, ate — in the monkeys' presence — its peculiar foods and then, when the afternoon grew late, departed. To the Professor it seemed that humanity had proved wanting in humaneness: the decency of decent citizens had betrayed the apes. The apes, inferior in species, were too little conscious to attend.

The Professor spoke to Percy, offering him the last fruit of his own observation of the rites — both mating and some others — of human beings.

66

"Homo Sapiens," he said, "took the wrong turning. He took it at some time in the dawn of history, at the moment when he decided to be a carnivore. At the moment when he found that killing was" — the Professor determined his adjective should be scientifically exact — "nicer than tilling."

He closed his eyes, and the impression of the dying sun, remaining in his eyelids, filled his whole field of vision with luminous, reeking bloodred.

He screwed up his face and his hands, and clung bitterly to the bars of the cage, hanging outside where Percy so often hung from the inside.

The red, fading from his eyelids, turned into a profound black.

He felt something leathery touch his palm. He opened his eyes and looked down. The monkey's forefinger had been inserted, to give comfort, in his own agonised fist.

"Could I," said a voice behind him, "trouble you for a light."

It was a clear, modest feminine voice, and the Professor's thought, startled and distracted, was, even before he turned round, that it could not this time be Kendrick.

She was a girl of gentle bearing, self-contained and well-bred, but not without vivacity; she wore one of those printed cotton dresses which, to the Professor's view, turned all women in summertime into girls of eighteen.

She proved to look a year or two older than eighteen; she had a lovely age, and it sat well on her, like her dress and bearing.

The Professor felt he was looking, rather clumsily, at Mozart's Susanna herself.

"Oh, certainly!" he answered. "Of course."

He took out his cigarette lighter, and Susanna leaned forward, balancing a cigarette in her mouth.

Holding the lighter in one hand, he shielded the flame with the other. There was no wind.

Percy, watching from a foot away but cut off by the bars, sighed: half the digestive sigh of an animal, half the conscious sigh of a thoughtful being. The Professor felt the exhalation on his arm, and could distantly smell the rank breath. The flame on the lighter went out.

The Professor, moving to shake the machine, saw that the girl's hand, comically disembodied in his view, caught in action as it might be by a camera, was supporting between its index and middle fingers his wallet.

He snatched at her wrist, and held it.

"What are you doing?"

"Oh, go on then," she burst out, "and call the police! You think yourself a great, strong man, don't you? Crime foiled again." Gentility and accent had collapsed. Susanna had left the stage, but the girl remained histrionic, and determined to get her plea in. "Just because I was brought up in an institution, and didn't know my mother, and never had a proper chance, and got into bad company, and got sent to borstal, and once you get in those places . . ."

Instead of pity he felt surprise that one who must have often made a professional appeal to pity should appeal so badly: unless the very amateurishness was meant to move.

"Why did you do it?" he asked.

"Well! Speaks for itself, doesn't it?" The girl looked down at the wallet still imprisoned between her fingers, as her hand was still imprisoned by his. Reminded, he slipped the wallet back into his pocket, not loosening his grip on her. "What do you want to carry all that round for? It isn't fair. It's putting temptation in people's way."

"You couldn't have known," he pointed out, "that it was full till you'd taken it."

"Oh." The girl was so crestfallen that he was, for the first time, moved. He saw she had believed her argument about temptation at the moment when she was speaking it.

Probably, he decided, the account of her life was factually true; but rather than remembering the life itself she had been remembering previous recitations of it, given, perhaps, on occasions like this.

"Why did you take it?"

"What's it got to do with you?"

"It's my wallet."

"So what? I've owned up, haven't I? What more do you want? I've confessed, haven't I?"

"You could hardly do otherwise."

"Oh, you sarcastic——" She twisted her arm away, but he held firm.

"Why did you do it?"

"Call the police."

"Why did you?"

She stared at him for a moment: then jerked her head with understanding. "Oh, I get it. You're one of them. Just my luck."

"One of what?"

"Trick cyclists, that's what they call them. Why, why, why — always on at you, till you can't call your soul your own. Why do you do this? Why do you do that? Well, I'll tell you why. Because" — she parodied the academic tone — "there was a basic emotional insecurity in my upbringing. Oh, I've met hundreds of your sort. And I can tell you none of them could do anything for me. Better psychiatrists than you have given me up. They said" — she parodied again — "I was not responsive to treatment. So now you know. And now you can call the police."

He made no comment.

"You *are* a trick cyclist, aren't you?"

Still no comment.

It made her uneasy. "What are you then?"

He thought which way of putting it would most impress her.

"I'm a professor," he said.

She was impressed: but she lunged back. "Absent-minded professor, eh? Well, I must say you do seem a bit preoccupied. Almost forgot to call a bobby, didn't you? Well, I'll give you a hint. There's one hanging about down there by that tunnel thing."

He didn't move.

"Go on," the girl said heroically. "I'm not squealing."

"What's your name?" he asked.

"Find out."

"I am doing. I'm asking you."

"And I'm not telling."

"All right. I expect the police will know."

"Gloria," the girl said.

"Oh. Gloria. A bit of a comedown," he murmured, "after Susanna."

"Who's she when she's at home?"

"Why did you do it?"

"Listen, you've no right to keep me here."

Looking round at the crowds, to whom they were, so far, no more than a man and a girl, he threatened her:

"I have only to say 'Stop thief' in a loud voice."

"Well if you insist on knowing," she said. "it made me feel funny being here."

"Yes?"

"I haven't been since I was a kid. They brought us once from the institution."

"And when you came here again?"

"Oh, I just felt to hell with everything. All these animals shut up. It doesn't seem right, really. I know they don't really feel anything, animals. But it reminded me of that place."

"The institution?"

"No no. Inside. Everyone locked in a cell. And being on show," she added, "for a lot of trick cyclists or professors or whatever you call yourselves to come and poke at. I just felt wild with everyone for doing it to me."

He was not going to be vanquished because she had by accident hit on his weak spot.

"But surely they don't lock you up in borstal?"

"Oh, I haven't just been in borstal. I grew out of borstal. I've been in prison."

"For picking pockets?"

"No! Breaking and entering. I've never picked a pocket in my life before today."

"That's why you're not very expert?"

"You *are* sarcastic. Anyone can see you're a teacher."

The second weak point.

"Are you satisfied now? Now you know all about it? Previous convictions and all."

"What difference do they make?"

"They'll get me a good long sentence — when you finally make up your mind to call a policeman."

"I don't think I'm going to."

She was certainly taken aback; he would almost have thought she was crestfallen again.

"Oh! Well! Well, ta very much. It's been nice knowing you. I'll move along now."

"Not so fast." He pulled her back.

"What is it this time?"

He must make up his mind, because it was cruel to keep the girl. The impulse of autocracy was strong: the feeling of the slave owner to the slave. The degrading attitude lurked in every decent citizen towards the gaol-bird; the attitude that she was a chattel, and so tarnished already as not to be worth cherishing. He must either relinquish her, or decide.

"I think there's something you can do for me."

"Me do something for you?" She was nastily mimicking a pretty surprise. "And what might that be?"

He was, to the depths of his soul, angry with the world. It took him a moment to cast off what he regarded as his obligation to act constitutionally: his civilised habit of mind had to be persuaded that it was right to express anger before he could surrender himself to the same chuckly, unscrupulous mood that had possessed him, the night before, in the bath.

"You mustn't ask me to do anything wrong," Gloria said. "If I get picked up, with my record, even if it's only on suspicion, it means a year. I don't want to do a year for you."

"You would be doing this," he said, planning it, "not so much for me as with me."

"Oh." Gloria's face fell flat, into resignation. "Oh — *that*."

In a moment he saw what she meant: the act which half Mankind called, either euphemistically, or through over-familiarity, or because none of its names expressed it, *that*.

The idea tempted him: the idea of forgetting monkeys and being, as the evening fell, soothed. *That* was the one interest which could oust all other interests.

Count Almaviva was not hard to understand. In youth, thinking of himself as an enlightened aristocrat, he had of his own free will abnegated his *droit de seigneur*. But in his middle age Susanna caught his eye. She was his servant. She herself had put the thought of *that* into his head by announcing her engagement to Figaro. How easy to go back on the generous impulse and act on the autocratic impulse: an impulse which delayed and bedevilled the wedding plans, and which it needed all Figaro's intrigues to overthrow.

The Professor did not regain his senses until he compared the girl not only with Susanna but with Percy: she resembled the ape in that she, too, had been imprisoned; she was bewildered and dependent; and she, too, stood in danger of being abused.

"No," he said, trying not to rebuff her willingness. "Not *that*."

"Then what?"

He looked round at the Zoo expecting the dusk.

"It's nearly closing time. Let me take you to supper, and I'll explain."

"I don't get it. What's in this for me?"

"Why, heavens girl — a free pardon. A free supper."

"I must say," Gloria remarked, "you can afford it."

"Perhaps also," he promised her as they walked away, "the redemption of your soul."

"I'll settle for supper."

II ESCAPADE OF A PROFESSOR

The Night,
Tuesday-Wednesday

THEY made their rendezvous in the depth of the night, under the boundary wall of the Zoo. Finding it easy to play on Gloria's sense of histrionics, the Professor had agreed they should synchronise their watches. Even so, she was a minute or two late, and he spent the interval feeling adrift, realising how useless he would be without the help of her expertise, and how unsure of himself without her companionship.

Suddenly she glided up and startled him. She had dressed herself in trousers. By what light there was — they were stationed as far as possible from any streetlamp — he could see the top of a metal tool stuck into the waistband. She wore a scarf round her head and had fastened it at the back, so that she looked like a pirate.

"All set?" she whispered.

"Yes."

"Let's go."

She sprang at the wall and managed to hook her arms over the top. She hauled herself up and the Professor heard her jump down on the far side.

As the man, and also the mover of the scheme, he was ashamed to lag. He leapt at the wall, but failed to hold on: he slithered down noisily, still on the same side, with a raw pain where he had barked his knees.

"Shh," said Gloria from the far side.

His stomach was constricted by the most gripping

of all physical fears, the fear of physical failure. Suppose the enterprise should be defeated because he could not scale the wall?

A yard or two along the road, a tree grew close to the wall. He examined it, and made a mental plan for climbing it. His limbs were overtensed and clumsy as he started on the way up.

The knots he had marked as footholds were slippery. The branches he had intended to clasp were out of reach; those he had intended to stand on creaked, and threatened to crack. In the end he found himself swarming the trunk, clinging desperately with both hands like a terrified rider clinging to the horse's neck. All dignity, all bravado was abandoned: he was only glad that Gloria could not see.

He reached a sufficient height, and considered transferring himself to the top of the wall. What he had planned as a single, easy step, now looked impossible. It was too far. He was swaying. It was too dark.

Rigid and cautious he got one hand over the gap; then the other. He jerked, gulped and took a chance, and brought his left leg across. He was leaning on two hands and a knee on the top of the wall; his muscles had frozen, and it seemed impossible his other leg would join him. He imagined himself stuck all night, waiting for day and, he presumed, the fire brigade.

Cautiously, he transferred the other leg.

"Come down," Gloria said urgently.

However, he was kneeling. His legs were imprisoned under him, held immobile by his weight. He could not jump from a kneeling position, and he could not see how he would ever reach a position from which he could.

"You can be seen," Gloria said. "Get down quick."

He felt it might have been a relief to be seen, and apprehended, once and for all. He planted his hands squarely beside him, and leaned on them. He felt his arms tremble.

He seemed to have no freedom, no room, to pivot; any movement would make him overbalance. Very slowly he twisted his body round, heaving his legs out from under him, squeezing and hurting them, until he was at last sitting on the wall, his legs swinging free, in Humpty Dumpty's posture.

He jumped down.

"I'm afraid," he began, "I'm not as young——"

"Don't talk so loud."

He realised he had been puffing.

"It all looks the same to me," she whispered. "You'd better lead the way."

He set off, shivering, but exhilarated by the success and secrecy of their entrance.

The Zoo was unfamiliar under the darkness. He took his bearings from the biggest edifices. The light of the setting moon was dim: it lay palely along rooftops and sometimes, as they passed unroofed enclosures, glistened on what might or might not be the form of an animal. He had the illusion he could hear the in and out breathing of a thousand sleeping creatures.

"Isn't it eerie?"

"No, no," he reassured her. "It's all right."

It was not eerie, but it was, he thought in an obsolete phrase, passing strange. Shaky after climbing the wall, unbelieving that the preposterous adventure was in fact taking place, he felt light with unreality. In the extraordinary silence, the Zoo appeared to him as if it had all been overwhelmed four thousand years before and preserved, petrified and empty. He might have been an archaeologist trying to decipher the purpose behind this reasoned, functional groundplan: but, even if the archaeologists of the future realised that here was a cantonment for housing and displaying the mystery of species, would it not seem to them wayward, a folly as inexplicable as the Labryinth of the Cretans?

He stopped short, seized by a dread that was perfectly earthly and present-moment. If it had been so hard to get in, how would they — the three of them — ever get out?

"What's the matter? Lost the way?"

He decided to postpone the question of exit, as he had already postponed the ultimate, absurd question whether his landlady would accommodate Percy.

"No. It's just here."

He led her round the corner; the angles of the buildings were smoothed by the dark.

"Is this the one?"

"Yes."

Gloria peered into the cage.

"I don't see any monkeys."

He explained the monkeys were in the back part of the cage, indoors, behind a hatch.

"Right."

She pulled the tool out of the waistband of her slacks.

While she worked at the bars, he admired her courage. He himself, standing at a spot which reminded him of the routine of his respectable life, was possessed by a hundred alarms and embarrassments. He felt furtive; his fancy projected encounters with attendants and policemen; he wondered how he would explain himself if he was challenged.

Gloria was not at all afraid, only excited. She must have dared the wrath of householders and police a hundred times. The Professor had been unable to find out more about her except that she was driven by resentment, which unwound itself not continually but by fits, moving on like the hands of one of those large, coarsely made clocks that jerked from minute to minute. When it jerked, she stole; in the intervals she was bored. Her progress was round and round the dial, repetitive and objectless; the fits of action interrupted any steady, respectable life she might have led. He was amazed by the power her resentment produced; the courage she had to cut herself off from all the security of the conventions and commit herself to this bold, lawless, commando independence.

"Wouldn't it be awful" — she giggled above the noise of her work — "if *all* the animals escaped?"

He was not sure that that was not, indeed, his dream, the logical replica of his present act of liberation on a large scale. The visionary exodus of the animals: it would be fantastic; it would also be anarchical. He knew that they would prey on each other, and on the city where he turned them loose; but he doubted if they would destroy as much as Man did. He was stirred by rebellion. It seemed axiomatic that all men were driven, though in different ways, by the same kind of engine; and therefore he would not hold the materialist who laid up treasure less to blame than the thief who broke in and stole. If he had visited Gloria's prison he would have seen it as the work not of justice but of injustice; he would have felt the same impulse to break open cells as he did to break open cages. If he had been taken on a tour of the Inferno, he would have felt none of Dante's resigned and pious pity; he would have had none of Dante's weeping in fear of his own skin: rather he would have rabble-roused among the damned, would have urged that their torments in mud or icy rain were torments of their own imagining, and that they were held fast by nothing except their own belief — their own unjustified belief — in their guilt; he would have ushered them up from their sunless circles to carry the gates by storm. That would be a tramping — the liberated march of elephant, petty thief and damned soul.

81

He heard a thin noise of snapping. "That's it," Gloria said.

He squeezed through the hole she had made and crossed the cage where, familiar as it was, he had never set foot before. He stooped, and rolled up the hatch.

Inside, it was warm, smelly and deeply dark.

Standing at the hatch, he called softly:

"Percy!"

Nothing responded. Kendrick could not have stolen him away in the night?

"Percy!"

There was a stir in the straw. Two feet from him he saw a pair of luminous eyes. He grew used to the dark and made out the greenish, furry head of the male monkey.

Beyond Percy, in the very recess, he could discern Edwina, asleep. She looked up for a moment. Without interest, she went to sleep again.

The Professor and the male monkey stared at each other. Forgetting that Percy knew neither words nor reason, the Professor whispered:

"Percy, come out — quietly. I'm going to take you home."

Percy stared a moment longer; then, disengaging his eyes, he looked past the Professor and saw the broken bar.

He vaulted through the hatch, knocking Darrelhyde away, crossed the cage, emerged, skipped over the path — "Stop him!" Darrelhyde shouted to Gloria when the animal had already passed her by — cleared a fence, vanished, and then came into view, outlined in moonlight, sitting still and intent on the crest of a sloping roof opposite.

The Professor clumsily made his way back through the cage. Squeezing between the bars, he stood poised to step down, and saw that Gloria was already climbing towards Percy. She reached the lower part of the roof. Crouched on the guttering, which did not look strong enough to hold her, she gradually straightened out, stretching the length of her body upwards, leaning on the slope of the roof.

The Professor was catching his breath.

Percy waited as the girl drew nearer. Her arms reached full extent; her fingers strained and crept up till they almost touched the monkey's toes. Percy sprang, at the last moment, to the further end of the roof.

"Come down," Darrelhyde called. "You'll kill your-self. And you won't catch Percy."

Indeed she would not; he remembered, now, the notes Hackenfeller had made about these animals' agility when they were free.

Gloria slithered down, and he met her at the foot of the building, their conference watched by Percy from above.

"What are you going to do now?"

"The animal is frightened," he explained. "After all, it hasn't much reason to anticipate good from human beings."

Ostentatiously standing clear of the wall, making it plain, he hoped, to Percy that he was not offering pur-suit, he called up in an unrestrained voice:

"Percy!"

"Haven't you got anything it would eat?" Gloria asked. "Perhaps we could tempt it down."

He searched his pockets for an apple. "No."

"You ought to have thought of it, really."

He walked away from the girl and called again, feel-ing foolish in the dark. He had some doubt now whether fright was the emotion that accounted for Percy's be-haviour. Percy confirmed the doubt. Finding a pebble on the roof, he dropped it on the Professor's head.

"Well?" Gloria demanded. "What do we do now?"

"I'm afraid there's nothing to do but wait. You could go home if you liked."

She thought about it. "No, it would be silly to go home now. What could I do at home?"

"Sleep," he suggested.

"No, I'll stay. If there was anywhere to sit, I could take a nap here."

"There's a bench." He led her to it, and they sat down where he had spent so many mornings. "When Percy's had his fling, he'll probably come back to his cage."

"It makes me feel queer," she said, "knowing that animal's loose."

"He won't hurt us."

"I shouldn't be surprised if I catch cold, though. It'll get chilly soon."

He took his coat off, and she wrapped it round her.

"You don't want me to watch for the monkey? I mean, I can go to sleep, can't I?"

"You can lean on my shoulder if you like."

She looked at him sideways. However, it was plain he had not changed his mind; he still did not want *that*. It was as well, she felt, that he did not, since he was so little attractive; but she was half insulted that he did not even try.

She laid her head on his shoulder and closed her eyes, while the Professor deliberately barred his mind to the impressions it received of her loveliness and her accessibility.

The past was so dim to his mind that it was almost a new experience to be free. He clasped his hands and swung his long arms up to the sky, exulting in the oiled articulation of his bones. Anchored by one giant, prehensile hand, he lowered himself to the guttering on the far side of the roof, and from there on to the ground, leaving the building between himself and the bench where the Professor sat.

Leaning clumsily on his knuckles, he crossed a path; then in a second he was airborne again, vaulting up another wall and up, on to a still higher roof. Exercise brought it back to him that he had once before enjoyed this athletic liberty: but the landscape that now lay beneath him was less monotonous than the jungle and seemed, as his vision penetrated the misty moonlight, more fruitful of mischief.

He travelled exaltedly, by roof, tree and fence. He came to a large circular pit, and jumped into it. In the middle, like a maypole, grew a single tall tree. He swung rapidly up and explored its branches, turning back the leaves with his fingers to find what was concealed there. He searched for a minute, and then uncovered the first animal life of his tour. Two Indian pandas, the colour of foxes and the shape of miniature bears, slept curled up in the branches. Percy gently blew into their snug fur, making a warm furrow: and then swung up, out, away, before they could wake and peer mutely into the night after him.

He passed like a substantial angel across the Zoo, touching off here and there the note of each species, as if he had been a child left alone in a concert hall with the deserted instruments of a full orchestra. Finding a sealion snoring on the bank of its pool, he rippled the water suddenly. He was a quarter of a mile away when he heard the responding bark. A peacock, feeling something move beside him, mistook Percy for his hen; forgetting his glory was lost on the darkness, he spread his tail and, passing a quiver through each quill as through links of chain mail, began his phenomenal rattling, unaware that he was making love to an ape. The Parrot

House was locked: but through the glass panel in the door Percy could make out a kaleidoscope view, dim in the moonlight, of varied, downy colours. He put his mouth to the keyhole, and jabbered. A macaw leapt on its perch, and shrieked. Its shriek set off the bird next to it; and the reaction passed down the house from cage to cage and perch to perch, until all the birds were awake, croaking and tuning up; and then, regaining their common sense, settling down with a flutter, they perceived it was still night and put off their harsh concert till the next day.

He entered the aquarium by the ventilator. Here was no noise, and only a little, greenish light. His soft feet made no sound on the tiles. He passed along the avenues, seeing in the tanks on both sides of him the outline shapes of silent activity, continuous through the night: an eel looping itself to and fro half buried in sand, and an octopus stretching and contracting its noise-absorbing tentacles. He sighed with wonder. Here was richness Africa had never shewn him.

Coming into the open air again, he ranged in many directions. He found himself in the Children's Zoo, in a pen full of domestic sheep. Forbearing to disturb them, he passed on to a corner where a rabbit hutch stood. Staring through the glass he focused such will-power on the rabbit that it woke and, seeing a monkey's face peering in on its privacy, squawked.

He bounded off, out of the enclosure, pursuing, like Caliban, his wondering, half-befogged, half-enlightened way.

Gloria did not intend to go to sleep. The excitement of adventure had quickly proved dull; as, indeed, it always did, like that other excitement of sex. It was imperative for her at once to disguise the flatness that had come over life; she must whip herself into taking an interest. Screwing up her eyes as she rested on the Professor's shoulder, she launched herself into a rigidly controlled daydream that she could rely on for the effect she sought.

First she must arrange what clothes she would be wearing. She decided on the very ones she had on now: only her trousers would be more fashionable. They would be of a kind she had long intended to buy — she minutely prefigured them now — tapered at the ankles. Those, with her headscarf, would give her an agile, freebooter appearance, which she perfected by hanging in fancy a pirate's ear-ring, single, gold, on the lobe of her right — no, her left — ear.

At first she thought the Professor's coat, draped on her shoulders, would complete the picture, accentuating her slimness. But the coat was shabby: and in impatience she erased the whole picture she had fantasticated so far.

Instead, she would be ensheathed in a slinky dress, rather metallic and heavy, low at the neck, sophisticated in cut, slit up the hem at one side.

Next, the man. He would be a mixture of Burt Lancaster and Marlon Brando. A chink of natural light broke into the mind she had so deliberately curtained off or, rather, had established underground, like a nightclub, so that it could be lit only by glamorous, artificial light. She could think of no name to give the man except Darrelhyde. She searched elsewhere: nothing came to her. She could feel the bony shoulder of the real Darrelhyde beneath her cheek. If she had to make use of his name she would take care he should be a Darrelhyde transformed.

He lolls against the mantelpiece. He is young but mature. He is twisted three-quarters round so he is almost turning his back to me, but I can tell he is not indifferent. His hand is in his trousers pocket. He says, between his teeth:

I could use a dame.

That so? I reply.

Like to come in with me? he says.

I look straight at him, half-smiling. He admires my cheek, I guess. He stiffens up and looks me all over; then, slowly, he moves a step nearer.

Behind my back my hand reaches for the door knob. My body moves away; my dress seems to get up and follow it a minute later. If anything, my face is now closer to his.

I have the door knob in my hand but I don't turn it.

I know what it will feel like if our lips meet. The tiny hard prickles of unshaven hair round his mouth, very slightly damp with sweat, will eat into my skin, his lips will be at the same time voluptuous and steel-hard, his teeth will force my mouth open ...

She did not want the dream to end so soon.

I break the spell. I got to be going now, I say.

You scared? he says.

Do I look scared? I say.

No. I guess you're not scared, he says.

Well, so long, rugged! I say.

What's the hurry? he says.

Oh, nothing. I guess our mob wouldn't be pleased to know I was alone with you at night in an empty house. That's all.

Who's the boss of your mob? he asks.

The difficulty of names broke in again.

Percy, I reply.

Swiftly, in order to oust reality, she elaborated the Percy of her fancy: Percy, fat, bald and, with his pink lips, repulsive; yet compelling; Percy ring-encrusted; Percy with wet cigar and lisp; racketeering in drink, drugs, gaming and pornographic pictures; immune, in his underworld empire, from the very thought of arrest, served by heavily-built, nerveless thugs obedient to his mere word on the blower.

Uh-huh, says the fantasy-Darrelhyde. So it's Percy. Not, he adds, a big-time operator.

He does all right, I say.

He did all right, says Darrelhyde softly. Until he met a bigger man.

When did he meet a bigger man? I drawl.

Tonight, says Darrelhyde. I shot him.

I make a tiny, indrawn gasp.

My eye travels boldly down Darrelhyde's long, taut thigh to his trousers pocket. I see that he is holding a gat there.

I part my lips, and shew him the tip of my tongue. If he embraces me now I shall be able to feel the gat pressing into my leg. He moves closer . . .

The real Darrelhyde shifted position a little. Gloria opened her eyes, and saw — after such a dream — the Professor.

She felt chilled and stiff from sitting on the iron bench. She had been tense with the effort of fantasy. It was the time of night when dew was forming. She was disappointed; dreams were futile; and a momentary image of what the Professor must look like unclothed caused her to shut her mind finally and imagine no more. She resettled her head and fell asleep. Her hair, where it protruded in a peak from the pirate scarf, became limp and pliable with dew.

From the top of a vast elm he could see the dawn come, slipping over the rim of the globe. Its blueish, dull, unshining light encroached in fingers on the distant reaches of the dark, like tidal water creeping up mud flats.

A reaction began to work in him which far predated his liberty. The obligation returned to mind which for a month past had gripped him from the first to last light every day. The memory of Edwina, imaged not so much visually as in his nostrils and his skin, was romantic and full of nostalgia. He became desirous of going back to her. How had he come to be so far from her at dawn?

He descended the tree and began making for his own cage.

He was travelled, triumphant, but also a bit hurried. He could not be sure that he knew the way back. He followed out the course he had had in mind, which he expected or, rather, hoped, would bring him to the cage. Instead it brought him to the sea-lion's lair. He turned away. Why had he ever thought it amusing to make the sealion bark? He tried another direction; and another; he was lost.

He sprang this way and that, no longer with any aim; eventually he lost hope. His heart was twisted by an image that would not leave his mind, that began to consume him, that persisted and swelled: the image of Edwina waking alone, betrayed by him she had waited for so long.

He found the cage when he had ceased to search; and he assured himself that it was home by the fact that two figures sat on a bench outside and the fact, which he had almost forgotten to believe, that one of the bars had been broken.

He sprang forward, and panic, frustration and dilemma resolved themselves in his only half-comprehending breast. The plot was unravelled; it was time for the last chorus of the last act; the right lover had found the right lover; sorting themselves out in the dusky garden.

The Professor was awake and stiff-eyed. He saw the monkey come but, knowing his purpose, made no move yet to trap him.

If Percy noticed the Professor it was only with passing fellow-feeling: there was the Professor with, in his turn, his girl. He pushed through into the warm inner compartment.

Edwina still slept in the straw, her back to the hatch. The light had not yet penetrated far enough to touch her eyelids. In her sleep she twitched and whimpered with discontent.

Percy laid his hand on her, gently, from behind.

She turned over and opened her eyes to a miraculous volte-face, Percy offering satisfaction to her long-held, honest sensuality. No questions disturbed her soul. Without modesty, she welcomed him home.

The light reached the inner cage and the Professor could, by creeping a little nearer, have witnessed what no white man had ever seen: half-dance, half-drama, the first work of art created by a species less than Man. However, he did not move from the bench, thinking at first that it was because he did not want to disturb Gloria: but as the light dawned stronger and he could have seen from where he sat, he found he had, in unscientific compunction, averted his eyes.

"Am I dreaming, or did I see that monkey go into the cage?"

"He went in a minute ago," the Professor replied.

"Aren't you going to catch him?"

"There's time enough. We can spare an hour or two."

"This damp won't do my hair any good."

He thought she had gone back to sleep. In a minute, however, hearing the rustle of straw, she said:

"What's he doing in there?"

91

Darrelhyde repressed the first word that came to mind. "Mating," he answered.

"Oh." Perhaps with cold, Gloria shuddered, and then giggled slightly. "Aren't animals *awful*?"

Wednesday: Sunrise

"So we *are* here. I thought it might all be a dream." She sat up straight. "Of all places to be. What did you want to get me mixed up in this for?"

"Surely this is better," he said, "than waking up in a cell?"

"At least you're warm there," she said.

"I'm sorry."

She drew his coat round her. "This thing's not bad, actually."

"I thought it was more constructive to bring you here than send you to prison."

"Suppose I don't want to be constructive?"

"Think what a strong moral position you're in now," he urged. "You've often broken and entered. This is the first time you've done it for someone else's sake."

"Oh? Whose? Yours, I daresay?"

"No, no! Percy's."

"Oh, him. What's he done for me?"

"How do you mean?"

"Haven't you heard that before?" she asked. "Everyone says it."

"What does it mean?"

"It means — well — why should I do anything for him?"

It was an odd position indeed: to be sitting on a bench in the sunrise discussing metaphysics with a thief.

"Now we are here," she asked, "aren't you going to get the monkey out?"

"Yes indeed. We'll — would you like to go home?" he asked.

"I might as well stay now."

"In that case — it will be a great help — we've got to get him home before there are many people about."

"We're going to look funny," she said, "dragging a monkey through the streets."

"He'll have to come willingly. He's too big to drag. I thought if you took one hand, and I took the other, he could walk between us — like a child."

"Well, get him out, anyway."

He called into the cage to waken Percy. There was a stirring and then Percy, curious, looked out of the hatch. Seeing the Professor, he came to him eagerly.

The Professor reached through the bars and took the monkey's hand.

He came out confidently. Gloria moved up to take his other hand, and for a second the animal hesitated, looking at the Professor for advice. Then he let the girl grasp him.

A soft chatter filled the Zoo: animals acknowledging the sunrise.

Suddenly, underneath the chatter, there was a deeper foreign noise. A gear shrieked, a mudguard scraped a wall. It was the first time Percy had heard a motor car.

He cast at the Professor the look of a person betrayed. He wrenched free, sprang over the path and then up, to where he had taken refuge before, the top of the opposite building.

"Percy! Come back! Do you hear me? Percy!"

The animal made no move. He was not being coy now. He was afraid.

"All you care about is that monkey! What about me?"

94

"You're all right," he said. "Just keep out of the way till the Zoo opens. Then you can walk out just as if you'd bought a ticket."

"What do you mean keep out of the way? How do I know where they're going to look?"

"They're coming to Percy's cage of course."

"Right. This is where I say ta-ta. You'd better take this." She swung his coat at him.

"Thank you." As he put it on the weight of the inner pocket assured him his wallet was still there. It had been at Gloria's mercy all night.

"Look," he said. "Let me give you some money."

"I haven't done anything."

"I could never have got that bar open without you."

"No, well, you wouldn't know how, would you? I mean, you haven't had my sort of life."

"Let me pay you. For professional services."

"For professional services!" She giggled. "I don't know if you're being sarcastic or if you're just funny."

"Let me give you——"

"No, thanks all the same. Bye-bye." She walked off.

He had no time to insist. "Percy!" he called up to the roof. "Percy!"

Percy crouched down and peered into the Professor's eyes, debating whether to trust him.

"Percy! Quick!"

He reached his hand up. Percy retreated a little way.

There were footsteps on the path.

"Make your mind up."

The monkey did nothing.

"Oh Lord!" the Professor said, still whispering. "Oh Lord! Well, if you won't come down, at least get out of sight. Make yourself scarce!"

Percy recognised this as a change of tactics. He could not understand the new instructions but he guessed their import. He was offended. He sat up stiffly on the roof.

"Shoo!"

Percy refused to budge. He stared brazenly at the Professor.

Awkwardly, the Professor began to flap his arms, as offensively as he could. "Shoo! Shoo!"

Percy realised that the first human being he had trusted was threatening him. He slid down the far side of the roof, cleared a fence and disappeared into the Zoo as into a maze.

The Professor dodged into the lee of the building which had lately been Percy's refuge, and the men appeared outside the cage.

Kendrick led. Immediately behind walked a man whom the Professor inexplicably recognised as an official of some sort, though he was wearing mufti. The boy who cleaned Percy's cage was in attendance behind them.

"Hullo! Look at this!"

It was the official who stopped short at the broken bar. Kendrick stepped economically into the cage and disappeared through the hatch.

He came back in a moment. "There's only one here."

"Which one?"

"The female."

The official looked round for the boy. "Tom! Get back to the office and give the alert."

"Keep your hair on," Kendrick said. "I want the boy to give me a hand first."

"Mr Kendrick, I carry some responsibility, and I intend to discharge it. Tom! Alert everyone to the effect that a dangerous animal is at large."

The boy was insolent. "Oh, go on! Percy wouldn't hurt a fly."

"A brute that can burst that bar," the official said, "would make short work of a fly. Anyhow, it's his mating season. You don't know what he may be like."

The conviction of crisis seemed to change Tom's bearing, almost his stature. He stood up lithe. His superfluous two inches of hair almost seemed to shear themselves.

He ran off, making a clatter on the path.

Kendrick was examining the bar. "I don't think our Percy did this. It looks pretty slick to me."

"You mean it was an intruder?"

"Profesional, I should think." Kendrick was grinning.

"Why should anyone steal a monkey?"

Kendrick shrugged. "They're worth a lot nowadays."

"Well, the man may still be somewhere around. I must get back——"

"Give me a hand with the monkey first," Kendrick said.

"What monkey?"

"What's her name?" Kendrick looked at the label. "Edwina."

"You can't take her. She's not yours."

"Mine wasn't delivered."

"You have no authorisation from the owner."

"Where's he? Africa, isn't he?"

"You have no legal right."

"I should have thought," Kendrick said, "you'd want to make sure I don't manhandle her. But if you don't care, I expect I can manage on my own."

"I cannot possibly consent," the official said.

"Who's to stop me?"

He was already in the cage.

The Professor had relied on the official, or whoever

came in his place, to take a stand on legal rights; but he had not supposed he would stand so weakly. He found himself forced to make a melodramatic move. He stepped out of the shadows.

"I am."

"Hullo," Kendrick said.

The official was startled.

Kendrick said, without hurry: "Don't you know each other? This is Professor Darrelhyde."

"I'd like to know what you're doing here," the official began.

"You can't take Edwina," Darrelhyde said, speaking only to Kendrick, "because she's pregnant."

"This sounds like a real meaty drama."

"Yes, I know. But it's true."

"You're sure you're not making it up, as a last desperate bid or something?"

"I give you my word of honour I have every reason under the sun to believe it."

"Blast," Kendrick said. "Well, I think I'll hang around a bit and see if Percy turns up."

"You'd better come to the office," the official said.

"Right. Anyone want a lift?"

They walked round the corner to where he had parked his shooting brake.

"I'm glad to see," the official said, "that though you may not respect the Law, the moral law is still alive in you."

"How's that?" Kendrick was unlocking the car.

"That universal feeling" — the official seemed to appeal to Darrelhyde as against Kendrick — "which prevents us, for example, from hanging pregnant women."

"Oh, that," said Kendrick. "No, it's not that." He got in at the driving seat, and opened the door on the other side for the official to get in. "You not coming?" he asked the Professor.

"No, thank you."

"Right." He lowered the window to talk through. "No, it's because pregnancy might upset our calculations."

"Your calculations?" the official queried, sitting beside Kendrick.

"We might think something was a space reaction when it was only" — he pressed the ignition button, and then turned to smile at Darrelhyde — "morning sickness."

In Prince Albert Road a policeman went from front door to front door: knocked: was, after a moment, answered: and in a calm conference delivered his calm warning.

There was no other sign. Office workers queued for and filled the buses. One or two children were accompanied to the playground who usually went alone. A couple of old ladies, out early to enjoy the sun before it became overbearing, carried umbrellas; but a temperament jittery enough to carry arms against an escaped monkey would also be jittery enough to carry arms, even on such a day as this, against rain; the umbrellas might have no other significance.

Tom, returning to the Zoo after visiting his home in Princess Road, found he had recaptured the spirit that had filled life in his childhood.

He had been an evacuee. The country town where he stayed was bombed on three successive nights and, one Saturday afternoon, machine-gunned from the air. There had been, not only on the days of actual danger but for a year afterwards, an infectious spirit, almost a genius, of crisis. It had stiffened Tom. Everyone at that time had helped everyone else. Everyone had refused to panic. Everyone seemed particularly alive, and even those who had been killed had not died tamely.

This feeling came back now as he patrolled the Zoo. The very shotgun he carried, which he had dug out from the attic at home, provoked memory. His father had taught him to use it — in case of parachutists.

Percy's first feeling was glad repudiation. He had exposed the Professor, at last, as an enemy. At last he was free from the moral pressure that had urged him towards something he could not comprehend.

He felt even freer in spirit than he had done the night before.

Then he began to tire of moral liberty as he had already tired of physical liberty. Physically, he was exhausted. The Professor had not let him have his sleep out; and that at first seemed typical of the Professor's nattering officiousness. He would have liked to go back to the cage and resume his sleep beside Edwina.

He reconsidered his judgement of the Professor. Why they had had to take such a form was a mystery, but he began to think that the Professor's actions, even his attack, had been for Percy's own good.

He hardly noticed that he was geographically lost because he was overwhelmed by the despondency of being morally lost. If he could only have found the Professor, and received instructions from him, he would have forced himself to the utmost to understand and obey them.

Even to Percy, who had never seen the place before by daylight, it seemed there was something amiss in the Zoo. He watched, bewildered, from above, as groups of people met and then parted, each taking a different track in what appeared to be a search. Concealed in the bosomy foliage of a tree he eavesdropped a council that was being held below, among strange men. Deaf to words, he went by gestures: and the sense of crisis which the men were studiedly repressing from their conversation was immediately betrayed to the animal.

He was on the point of descending to join them, undeterred even by the fact that he did not know them. He was scared off by the evidence that they themselves were afraid. He would be as safe with them as if he had handed himself over to a stampede of elephants.

He clambered off; and from every high point on his aimless route he searched for the Professor. His mind grappled with the idea that he had thrown away a chance. If he had trusted, he would have been in the Professor's company now. He climbed the highest tree in sight and looked, forlornly, in every direction.

A long way off, at the far end of a broad concrete strip, he saw someone who, though it was not the Professor, was recognisable, though Percy could not place him precisely.

He came swiftly to the ground. Then, throwing his arms wide, roaring with joy, and making the tremendous effort it took for him to run upright, he surged towards the man in order to give himself up.

In the face of the charge, Tom maintained a perfect competence. He noticed that his muscles did not hesitate. The joy of sharing a manly pursuit with his father came back; he remembered all the lessons; and took aim now with classic correctness.

The monkey dropped. Without pain he remembered the assembly of animal shapes that had been presented to him the night before, though he could not now tell if the experience had had any reality. It came to him that all these kinds of creature could, though he had no time to work it out, be arranged as a progressive series. It must have been with the idea of adding to, perpetuating or improving that series that the Professor had exhorted him to try and try, to seek something that had always been just past the horizon of his understanding.

He thought happily of Edwina. He had satisfied her, and in doing so had passed on the burden the Professor imposed on him to some other life, at present budding and fermenting in Edwina's belly. Percy had done his part. He had no more personal obligations. He had pleased the Professor.

The Professor occupied the last and most enduring image in his dying mind. There came a revelation, profound and piercing. He was filled with a sense of privilege as he recognised what, though he had been blind to it at the time, had graced his life with its presence these last weeks. The Professor was Super Monkey. On his pattern Percy, Edwina and all the other lesser monkeys in the Zoo were modelled.

Once recognised, the deep truth of this made it obvious in a hundred ways. How else to explain the Professor's wrinkled face, his loping walk, his stoop, his bowed legs and dangly arms?

The last proof, confirming as it did that the Professor, no matter how mysterious, was benevolent, made the monkey think he was smiling to himself with heavenly serenity, though in fact his muscles were paralysed and he could not change his facial expression. Super Monkey, he thought, unlike ordinary monkeys, covered himself with clothes. That was because his body was so beautiful, so bright, that — this the Professor knew, in his tender concern — to reveal it naked would have dazzled Percy's eyes.

Wednesday Morning

THE Professor made his way through the mortuary and found himself looking down upon a pink, a completely skinned, Percy.

"Who did this?"

"A gentleman called Kendrick asked me to, sir. I hope I wasn't wrong to do it? Mr Kendrick said the monkey was his property."

"That's quite true. What's he done with the pelt?"

"He took it with him, sir."

"What did he want it for?"

"He didn't say."

"How long ago did he leave?"

"I should say about a quarter of an hour."

"Do you know where he was going?"

"He said he had to get back to Northolt, sir, in a rush."

It proved possible to open the Zoo on time, and presently there was a crowd for Gloria to mingle with. She could have made her way out unnoticed. However, she had no desire to leave: what should she do outside? On the other hand, what was there to do here?

Neither animal nor human diverted her. The people seemed for the most part middle-aged; they did not take her fancy and many of them were encumbered by children. She saw a few young men, but none she would look at twice; they were all young fathers, dragging unsightly children, and she could see in them already the unexciting look of domesticity.

As for the animals, she was out of sympathy with them. An animal could not talk. She bore it no ill will but it did not amuse her.

Even when, from the crowd's comments, she gathered that an ape had been shot, she was not moved. She presumed the animal was Percy, and from what she had seen of his perverse behaviour she guessed he had asked for destruction. There was no need to pity him because animals felt nothing. She was even pleased he had died, when she remembered what it was he had done in the dark inner compartment after — pretending to be submissive — he had come back there.

In the broad walk by the tunnel a knot of people stood, bewildered rather than excited. The policeman who patrolled the walk, and whose threat to Gloria no longer held good, tried without effect to move them on; but from time to time a straggler broke away of his own free will, either because he could not make out what was going on or because there was nothing to see.

Without much hope that it would interest her, Gloria pushed through and identified a couple of men in the middle of the group as small-time reporters. She had seen their kind often enough in court, and knew them to be dingy little men, more concerned with work than thrill.

Tom was looking at the ground and could feel rather than see that the crowd which had collected about him was beginning to break up. He hoped that would give him more air. The carcass had long ago been removed, and the mess cleared. Tom had put his gun down with the intention of helping shift the body; but, suddenly feeling sick, he had refrained and was grateful to be told that he need not come to the mortuary. The gun still lay on the ground.

He had been expertly questioned by reporters, who had now apparently received their fill, and inexpertly questioned by casuals who were disappointed to find him sullen and the ground washed. One or two women, all in or past middle-age, had come up to him and, looking as if they were about to stamp on his foot, accused him of being a brute. With the first he had argued. She shouted him down and flounced away. The others he had scarcely heard, concentrating all his forces inward in the effort to keep his gorge down.

A fair and probably pretty girl edged up to him; but his view did not rise above her legs, which were concealed by trousers.

She asked, in a voice faint because she was drawing in her breath:

"Are you the one that shot him?"

He expected some further sentimentality.

"Yes."

"Golly," she said. "You must be brave."

He raised his head, and they looked at each other.

Gloria felt a familiar frisson: the beginning of yet another cycle of adventure.

To Tom the feeling was new, and it seemed to him the culmination of his nausea.

"Come off it," he said.

"No, honestly."

He realised he had clicked with a girl. He began to phrase invitations. He was entirely free, to date her or not to date her; it all rested with him. Yet he was embarked, beyond any going back, on a compelling stream; the swelling nausea in his throat and stomach was exciting and almost pleasant. He knew he would, definitely would, date her: and it was in the sense of doom that the pleasure existed.

The driver pushed back the glass panel behind him, and said:

"This is Northolt."

"Oh. Oh, well." The Professor moved to the front of his seat. "Do you know Northolt at all?"

"It's out of my area."

"This place I'm looking for isn't the airport but it may look something like it. It might be in the same district. It will be some sort of establishment — a group of buildings, I suppose — with fields attached."

"There's lots of fields round here."

"Yes, I know. These fields will be a sort of launching site."

"There's something about half a mile along this way that they call the experimental station."

"That'll be it."

"Do you want to go there?"

"Yes, of course. Quickly."

They turned off the main road into a rutted lane bordered with thick hedges. Thrown up by a bump, the Professor glimpsed over the top of the hedge to his right a rising expanse of grass like a down. On the ridge of it, tiny in the distance, stood — like a prehistoric monument — something which looked like an elongated egg, standing in an elongated egg-cup. It flashed out of sight; but the Professor had noticed that it cast a boiled-egg shadow curving over the crest of the hill, and that it must, seen close to, be enormous.

"That's it!"

They drove to the end of the lane and drew up before a wire gate. On the right stood a dark-brown, tarred wooden hut.

An old man, presumably an old soldier, wearing a

black uniform of no particular significance, came out to them.

"Look here," the Professor called through the taxi window, "I want to see the director of this establishment at once."

"May I see your papers please, sir?"

Too tired to bother with normal conversation, the Professor spoke his thoughts.

"How very Continental. I'm afraid I have no papers."

"I can't let you in without papers."

"I don't want to go in! I want you to bring the director out here. You must have a telephone in your hut?"

"I can't get through to headquarters without seeing your papers, sir."

"This is very urgent indeed."

"You must see my point, sir. If I did that, anyone could come up here from the village and ask to see the controller."

"Wait a minute." The Professor took out his wallet and gave the man his visiting card.

"You a boffin, sir?"

"I've heard that word somewhere but I can't place it. Perhaps it was in some film."

"Well, I'll ring through."

The Professor sat on in the cab. The driver asked:

"You want me to wait?"

"Yes. Of course. We may be fetching someone away from here."

The old soldier returned.

"He'll be along in a minute, sir."

"Good. Good. Thank you."

"Would you like to wait in my lodge?"

"Thank you."

The Professor pulled up the handle of the door and

found he was pressing against a strong force of wind. He pushed the door open and was blown upon, as he descended, by a warmish, dry tornado, an unnatural wind that might have come from a desert. The cab door slammed before he could close it. The sunshine seemed unabated: yet he hoped — if only it would come in time — that the wind might presage a change of weather. It subsided as he stepped into the hut.

He waited some time.

"No. I wouldn't trouble him again," the old soldier said. "He doesn't like me to be always ringing through."

The taxi driver tramped over to them.

"Are you sure you want to keep me?"

"Yes, if you can possibly stay."

"The meter's ticking over, you know."

"I'm not in my dotage. I can control my own money."

"Want to come in here?" said the old soldier.

The taxi driver refused, and went back to his cab.

The Professor nearly fell asleep. He wondered if it was not in excess of his obligation to come so far and wait so long, when he was already fatigued by a night's vain activity.

He jerked awake; and a middle-aged, firmly-built man had approached.

"Professor Darrelhyde?"

"Yes."

"Well, now. What can I do for you?"

"You must stop that rocket."

"What rocket?" The man's face remained affable, bland, without reaction.

"Oh, don't try your tricks on me," Darrelhyde said. "You know as well as I do. Kendrick's rocket."

"Mm. It certainly appears that Security's slipped up."

"Stop the rocket. There's a phone here. Stop it at once."

"Why?"

"Because Kendrick's inside it."

"You think so?"

"I know he is. Now will you stop the thing?"

"I can't. It's gone."

"You mean it's disappeared? It's been stolen?"

"It'd be a big thing to steal. It was launched" — he looked at his watch — "about fifteen minutes ago."

"While I was here?"

"I suppose so. Yes."

"Why couldn't you come at once?"

"I could hardly desert my post — could I? — at zero hour."

"I didn't hear anything." Darrelhyde said.

"Didn't you feel what you probably thought was a gale and a half?"

"Was that it?"

"Since half the countryside probably felt it, there seems to be no harm in telling you. Your friend Kendrick will probably tell you anyway."

"Kendrick's in the rocket."

"Don't be a fool. There was a monkey inside it." He stopped short. "Who are you pumping anyway? Oh well, I suppose I've let that one slip, so if it will set you at rest I'll go on and tell you that there was a monkey and nothing else in it."

"Kendrick was inside the monkey."

"Mm. Like Jonah."

Rocky with tiredness, the Professor said deliberately: "He was inside the monkey's skin. It was only skin. The rest was Kendrick."

"Are you serious?"

"Very."

"No, look here, I saw the monkey myself, going into the rocket."

"How close were you?"

"I had binoculars."

"Did you notice the way it walked?"

"Actually, I didn't look very hard. To tell you the truth, I think it's a pretty poor show to use animals. I never like it. You probably think that's soft."

"Not in the least." The Professor felt too weary to be more than polite. "But in this case, as I've told you, it wasn't an animal."

"You really are serious, aren't you?"

"Presumably you can verify it."

"Yes. Of course. But Good Lord! Good Lord! Kendrick was inside the monkey!"

"He's a very brave young man," the Professor said.

"He's a darn' lucky one!" The man began to laugh. "Good Lord! What a thing! How did he get away with it?"

"By being short," Darrelhyde said. "It's the only flaw in him."

"The ingenuity of it! I'd never have thought of such a thing."

"What are his chances," the Professor asked, "of coming down safe?"

"It would infringe Security if I told you."

"Does it matter now?"

"Not much."

"Then tell me what you think, professionally."

"It'll be a shaky do."

Darrelhyde felt his patience or simply his power to stay awake was being exhausted before his sympathy. "I'm an old pedagogue," he said. "Couldn't you tell me straightforwardly, in such a way that I shall understand, whether Kendrick will come back alive?"

"He won't," the man said.

Even before the need to eat came the need to sleep.

But before he could sleep he must bath: his eyelids were creaking with rheum, his feet gritty; his limbs ached from being drenched in their own sweat, and sweat had bodied out his clothes like starch.

At the bathroom door stood his landlady.

"I thought you'd soon make your way back here."

"A bath," he said, "doesn't last for ever. It has to be renewed. So of course I've come back."

"Have you been drinking?" she said. "Is that where you were all night?"

"Why do people use the past continuous, or rather the perfect continuous I suppose it is, in preference to the adjectival past participle?" He could hear his voice pegging on. He was not interested in what he was saying but he could not stop. "Why is it so much worse to have been drinking than to be drunk?"

"Then you admit it?"

"By no means. I may be intoxicated but it is only with cares."

"At least you haven't lost your sense. You've got enough wit left to come creeping back like I knew you would——"

"I am not creeping. I want a bath, but I am not trying to take it surreptitiously." The whole episode appeared to him like a colourless and only distantly unpleasing nightmare. His landlady was upset; he could hardly focus his mind on discovering why. "I realise that midday is an unconventional time to take a bath——"

"Midday! It's nearer three."

"Is it so late?"

"Yes it is! It's too late! You needn't think you can slip back now and rub it off before anyone sees——"

"Rub what off?"

"The drawing. It was you, wasn't it? The drawing on the soap?"

111

Leaning on the wall in the corridor he managed to remember, and laughed. "Oh yes. That was me."

His confession made her less angry. "Well, Professor, I know that gentlemen do have some funny ideas, especially when they reach a certain age, but there are ladies in this house."

"Yes, of course."

"I suppose you stayed out all night because you were afraid to come home. And so you got drunk."

"Honestly, I'm not drunk."

"Then you were cheeky to me, Professor, which is just as bad isn't it? I'm afraid you'll have to leave us, Professor."

"Oh yes, of course," he said. "I'll pay my rent up. Then I can leave at once."

"If you've nowhere to go——"

"My sister will put me up."

"Oh, yes. You've got a sister, haven't you?"

"Yes. I'll pack as soon as I've had a sleep and a bath. I take it I may have a bath?"

"Of *course*." She smiled at him. They seemed almost to be in good accord.

He began to count out the notes from his wallet.

"No, no," she said. "I don't want to trouble you now. Any time will do."

"Will nobody disembarrass me of this money?" he said. He forced her to accept it.

In the bath, his head kept nodding forward so that he was afraid of falling asleep and being drowned. He tried to focus his eyes through the dancing steam, on his boiled, scraggy body.

"Professor!" His landlady was tapping on the door and speaking sweetly. "Professor! Telephone!"

It was Post. "Look, Darrelhyde, did you have an accomplice?"

"An accomplice?"

"Did anyone help you cut that bar?"

"You know about that?"

"Of course. I just want to know if anyone helped you."

"No, I was alone."

"Funny. I'd never thought of you as a handyman. The police almost thought it was a professional job."

"Have they been called in?"

"I've spent half the day persuading them it wasn't in your nature to drag anyone else into a business like that."

"Did you convince them?"

"Oh yes, I'm sure I did. In fact, I think we've hushed it up pretty smoothly all round."

"Thank you."

"I'm only sorry I couldn't do more. You realise you'll be suspended, don't you?"

"Shall I?"

"The Faculty feel——"

"That I'd better lose my job?"

"You need a rest, you know. You were in quite a state when I saw you on Monday. I don't think I did you any good, either."

"I don't honestly think you made any difference," Darrelhyde said.

"I'm not so sure. The Victorians repressed the facts of life. We repress the facts of death. I may have shocked you."

"I'm not as delicate as that."

"I'm not so sure. I blame myself a bit," Post said. "It may have shocked you to realise you're blood-guilty like the rest of us."

"As far as last night is concerned," said Darrelhyde, "I take the whole responsibility. For the whole episode and all its consequences."

"I'm glad you seem a bit calmer. I hope you'll take a rest now."

"I'll be staying with my sister if you want me."

"I don't see that we'll need to disturb you."

"I might move into the country, though there's one thing I must see about first. I could move next year."

"Some of these provincial university towns are very nice."

"Are they?"

"You won't have any trouble getting a new job, you know. We're not dismissing you, or anything."

"I thought I might have a change."

"It would do you a world of good. There was this original research you were doing. You'll have leisure to write it all up now. I advise you to publish it. It makes a lot of difference. You'll find you'll have the pick of the appointments."

"I shan't be writing it now."

"Oh, you mustn't feel like that."

"It's not a question of feeling. I haven't got the facts."

"You haven't? But I understood the monkey did——"

"The monkey did his part. I didn't do mine."

"But it would have made your name!"

"I know."

After a pause, Post said:

"Darrelhyde, you do seem to have made a mess of this. Nothing saved at all. No monkey. No research. You seem to have made a total fiasco."

"I'm not sure. It may be nothing but a fiasco. It all depends on whether Edwina really is pregnant or not."

"But I understood — that man from the Zoo told me — he said you told Kendrick, in his presence — you told him authoritatively——"

"I told him that I believed it. I do."

"But you had nothing to go on?"

"Faith."

"It's too early for you to be sure?"

"At the time I gave my opinion to Kendrick, the pregnancy was some three hours old."

"Then, his calculations——"

"It couldn't," the Professor said, "have upset his calculations in the least."

III SOLILOQUY OF AN EMBRYO

Easter, The Following Year

It lay, a snug, smug, self-sufficient little incubus, in the middle of warm, wet darkness. Its legs were looped up in front of its chest, as if hooked by the knees; its back was curved like a prawn; its paws dangled — no use to anybody, satisfying only its own static comfort — before its nose; its eyes, never yet unsealed, consisted of two puckered slits.

It was strategically placed. Without expending any energy in achieving its design, it had managed to lie astride Edwina's internal lines of communication. It intercepted her food supplies. Whatever entered her body that could be useful, whether oxygen or nourishment, the embryo diverted to itself.

It took from her far more than it needed to maintain its quiescent, dark-enfolded life. It took without thought for her: its plundering was limited only by its power to consume. On the proceeds it grew larger; and this increased its capacity. It took more still. Edwina in consequence was always hungry. The voracity of the embryo outstripped even the increased rations fed to her by the authorities.

The embryo stored up the surplus food in fold upon fold of lardy flesh that had never seen the light of day. It grew swollen and gross. A need to take exercise came upon it, not for any altruistic or utilitarian reason, but simply to ease itself; the same need might have fallen upon an over-bloated epicure. Very slowly and heavily, like an unwilling child forced to perform on the bar in the gymnasium, it turned a somersault. It was now suspended head down.

It had, however, no conception of its position. It did not even know that it was inside something, still less that beyond that something lay a whole universe. When Edwina, very lumbering these days, moved, the embryo felt a special sensation, but hardly a sensation of moving; it knew as little about moving as if it had been sealed in a space-rocket.

Edwina's lurchings were rather discomfortable to the embryo. They tended to nauseate its over-fed body. It discouraged its environment from moving by lying as heavily as it could, its great stone-like skull hanging down like a dead weight.

Edwina, trying to reach a position of comfort in relation to the weight within, shifted from side to side as she lay. The embryo, concerned only for itself, resisted with all its inert force.

The new head-down position left it more room to expand. It found it could take more than ever: it began to sop up all that came to it. Presently it found that it was not only at bursting point within its own skin; it was also over-filling the cavity allotted to it. The surrounding walls could stretch no further. At the last point of elasticity, they were pressing in on the enormous embryo.

Now it felt more than a simple need to exercise in order to regain comfort. It had not assimilated all the inflowing food. Indigestion gave it a bad temper. For the first time it felt spiteful. A desire came to it to injure the tissues of its warm, damp prison which was involuntarily pressing so hard. It screwed its knees up to its chin, coiling-in all the energy it had so long stored: and then lunged with its first attack on its mother's inside.

"It's for you."

The Professor dreamed it was his landlady calling him; then woke to realise he was staying with his sister. It was only just light.

The voice on the telephone was incoherent.

"Oh, Professor, is that you? I'm sorry to wake you so early. Thank God you're still in town."

"Who is that?"

"Tom."

"I'm sorry. I don't——"

"It's Tom, Professor! From the Zoo!"

"Oh, Tom. What do you want?"

"Professor, it's coming."

"Don't be silly. It isn't due."

"I know it isn't. But there's no doubt about it, and I couldn't think of anyone to call except you. Please come right away, Professor."

"I thought they'd fixed up with some vet or other."

"He's away over the holiday. He didn't expect it yet. You must come. I haven't a clue what to do."

"Well, heavens above, nor have I."

"Oh, you know all about animals, Professor."

"As a biologist, man. Not as a midwife."

"You can't leave me alone. Something will go wrong if you do."

"Where are you speaking from?"

"The Zoo. I daren't leave her. I can't get hold of anyone because of the holiday. She's sort of groaning."

"Oh Lord. All right. I'll come along."

"I don't know how you'll get in, Professor. I can't leave her while I come to the gate."

"I'll climb in," he said.

121

After the first kick, it lay back, relieved, listening to the effect of the injury it had done. It heard the snap of half a dozen minute capillaries, and then the slow infusion as bruising crept over the area. Smashed cell walls were carried away like débris in a river, banging against the sides of the blood vessels. It heard a gasping, half-smothered pulsation from the cells as they fought to take from the influx of nourishment sufficient to recoup themselves.

These sounds were so satisfying that the embryo began at once to plan, and to reserve energies for, another kick.

It seemed, after it had been kicking for some hours, that it had kicked once too often. This time the effort of the cells was not to renew their substance but to seal it off. In the dark, the embryo was surrounded by a continuous crackling and popping of cellular activity. It became clear that the damp stickiness of his environment, instead of pressing back upon him, was receding and withdrawing itself from vulnerability.

He thought he had won a victory.

Even as he thought he had overcome the tight fit, a new and ferocious pressure gripped him on all sides. He found he was being squeezed beyond all bearing, squeezed almost to death. Gulping and puking, he recognised that this pressure was actually dislodging him.

For the first time he was conscious of movement: and this was movement not according to the mobility of his environment but movement within it and in a different direction from it.

The pressure relaxed.

He had the awful sense of having gone, irrevocably, too far. The body he had assaulted was preparing to void itself of him. His jailer was willing to let him go free, and was even helping him on his way.

The pressure descended again. He clung on, too

tightly held either to resist or comply, capable only of enduring and, narrowly, surviving. It loosened, and he was lying a little lower down, exhausted.

It was his own fault. If he had not lain there selfish and full of appetite, he would never have grown too large to be carried, and could have stayed for ever. A revolting guilt seized him; mixed nauseatingly with sentimental nostalgia. How could his mother expel him? He did not want to go. He was afraid of whatever adventure might lie outside: for him the warm wet darkness was home, and sufficient. He wanted to stay where he was or, rather, not where he was now but further in still, where he had been a moment before in the immediate, but already unrecapturable, past. He began to scramble up again, urged by panic, levering, pulling, scratching a way back to where he had come from.

His scramblings, unmindful as he was of the hurt he caused, called down a further spasm of pressure upon him.

When it eased, he was lying still lower down and was full of resentful anger. He had done nothing to deserve this from his mother. With the retaliatory hurtfulness of a guest finding his departure speeded, with the pride-recouping unkindness of a lover answering "If you don't want me I certainly don't want you," the embryo convinced itself that release was what it had always sought; that it was, in manly fashion, impatient of this unexciting security and that its dearest desire was to be launched into the adventurous world.

Yet, if this was true, the embryo did not act rationally and simply on its desire. It did not slip, as it could have done, directly into the world; but, as the final spasm began, it determined that in its passage it would, to the utmost of its power, rend, lacerate and wreak spite on the mother who could no longer bear its chubby residence within her.

There were no buses yet but he found a taxi. Driving up Great Portland Street, he noticed that the windows of the shops were full of Easter lambs and Easter chickens, and he realised that Post would put this down to a survival, in the modern world, of sympathetic magic; Post would say that Man, in making these effigies of animals he ate at his feasts, was ensuring the perpetuation of his food supplies.

The taxi was held up at the traffic lights and the Professor, impatient, gazed at Soane's lovely, isolated church.

They drove on, up Albany Street, and then turned off towards the Zoo. He asked the driver to put him down. He was again delayed, looking furtive in his anxiety to look innocent, while he waited for the cab to turn round and drive away.

Alone in the empty road, he sought out the tree he had climbed before. Some of its knots were prickly with new spring growth.

He found Tom kneeling in the straw in the inner compartment of the cage. Edwina was still in labour. The Professor groaned as she groaned, and sweated as she sweated. He felt clumsy; and Edwina, from whom, despite her travail, he might have sought instructions, was without the use of words.

When there was a pause, the Professor asked Tom:
"Do you still see Gloria?"
"No. We stopped going together ages ago."
The constrictions began again.
"I wasn't flash enough for her," Tom added.
The young monkey in its fury inflicted on itself as well as its mother a rough delivery.
"What happens now?" Tom asked. "This?"

"I suppose so."

The nerves of its skin were already resentful of the chilliness of atmosphere. Now it was painfully and finally severed.

The park outside smelt drenched and vernal. It was sodden from a fall of rain, and its verdancy was enhanced. A cool sunshine was beginning to appear.

A few people were already about. Moving between the trees, they gave variety to the raw greenness.

Lying in the straw, he seemed marked already as one of the inadequate who would not survive. The violence boiling in him as a result of his undignified birth would, it now appeared, be turned against himself. To spite his mother he would commit suicide by refusing to breathe.

The Professor, infuriated for Edwina's sake that her pain should go for nothing, picked him up roughly.

"You'll kill it, Professor," Tom said. "You'll kill it."

There was, however, a sign that the young monkey would live, and, in the effect it made on the rest of the Zoo, an indication that it would take after its father. It woke all the other animals and set them gibbering as it let out its first roar of wrath.

THE END